THE HOG LADY

ALSO BY JOHN A. RUSSO

The Darkest Web

The Night They Came Home

The Unearthly

Weep No More

Etta

The Killer Next Door

Dead Lives Matter

Day Care

Inhuman

The Sanity Ward

Passion, Pleasure, and Pain

Simon Rocail Novels

The Price of Admission

Paranormal Obsession

David Cristi and Vito Martinelli Mysteries

The Killing Truth

The Killer and the Movie Star

THE HOG LADY

JOHN A. RUSSO

WOLFPACK
PUBLISHING
—— EST 2013 ——

Wolfpack Publishing
9850 S. Maryland Parkway, Suite A-5 #323
Las Vegas, Nevada 89183

wolfpackpublishing.com

Paperback ISBN 978-1-63977-996-3
eBook ISBN 978-1-63977-596-5
LCCN 2023944306

THE HOG LADY

Based on a true story

1

Jackie Kelter didn't believe that a restraining order would actually protect her. She had obtained it out of fear and desperation. She knew that resorting to "legal protection" was often the precursor to an untimely death at the hands of an abuser.

Bradley was supposed to drop their two kids off at precisely twelve noon today, and after that, he would be under strict orders to stay away from her apartment. But he was not a man who could be easily thwarted by rules and regulations of any sort. Now she was *more* scared of him, not less.

Prior to the protection order, he had relentlessly harassed her with obscene phone calls and vicious threats tucked under her windshield wipers. He had slashed all four tires of her automobile, and she knew it was his doing even though she couldn't prove it. He had left a dead rat on her front porch, wrapped in a pair of her panties that he must have taken from one of her dresser drawers before she moved out. Jackie had shown the rotting animal corpse to the police and had pleaded for protection against Bradley, who had repeatedly warned her that if she ever left him, he would track her down and kill her, but the police said an assault had to actually be committed before they would have grounds to make an arrest.

Great! Jackie had thought. *You'll punish him after I'm dead!* She wanted to believe that Bradley wouldn't kill their three children, and he had never said that he would. She didn't want to die, but she hoped he'd kill only her.

She had married Bradley Kelter seven years ago when she was only eighteen. She started dating him when they were both juniors in high school. He was a football player, and she was a cheerleader. They weren't the stars of their squads, but they were still envied by most other students, an adolescent celebrity status that they both basked in. But she got pregnant three months before they graduated, and they got married four months after they got their diplomas. She went into her marriage with a determination to make the best of it, but he started insulting her and slapping her even before their first child was born. She wanted her baby to have a father, so she stayed with him as his emotional and physical abuse got worse and worse. He had no special skills, so he worked menial jobs, and when he wasn't working, he was usually drunk. The money they should have used to pay bills mostly went toward his booze habit. Meantime, she had two more children.

One night she woke up to him sexually assaulting her in her bed, with his hands around her throat. She fought him off, somehow squirming out from under him, and told him that what he was doing was rape. "Rape?" he jeered at her. He told her he would show her what it was really like to be raped, and he threw her back onto the mattress. She bit his hand as hard as she could when he clamped it over her mouth. He started strangling her. Then their four-year-old daughter came into the bedroom and yelled at him to stop hurting Mommy. He pulled his pants up and staggered into the bathroom, and slammed the door shut.

Jackie phoned 911 and when the police came, they believed Bradley when he claimed she liked "rough sex" so he was giving it to her. He said she liked it that way even when she pretended not to, which made it hard for him to exactly know when to stop. The police officers grinned and chose to believe him. In the end, she refused to press charges because she felt so helpless and intimidated. She even felt guilty, as if she had done something to deserve what he had done to her. As if she must not be skilled enough for her husband in bed.

She endured her miserable marriage for five more years before she got up the nerve to see a psychologist who offered pro bono counseling for abused women. Gradually she began to become more aware of her self-worth until she finally was motivated to file for a divorce and appeal for custody of her three children. To her great surprise, her lawyer prevailed by finding a witness against Bradley, a young woman with whom he had been having an affair, and she willingly testified that he had also been abusing her. Jackie was shocked to find all this out, but she was also glad that it had ended up working in her favor. Bradley was granted limited visitation rights along with occasional weekend custody. But of course she still wasn't totally free. She was filled with dread every time she had to deal with him.

———

BRADLEY KELTER, scruffy and unshaven and with a mean look in his eyes, drove his Jeep down his ex-wife's tree-lined street and parked in front of the shabby little bungalow that she was renting. When he got out of the Jeep, he reached under the front seat to pull out a long, sharp knife, which he concealed under his denim jacket. Furtively he looked all around, hoping he'd be lucky enough not to be seen by Jackie's neighbors as he crept onto her front porch and knocked, keeping his face in the shadows under the eaves.

Jackie opened the door, and it seemed to him that she had gotten better looking after she divorced him. Or maybe he just desired her all the more. She was a petite brunette, barely over five feet tall and weighing a hundred pounds soaking wet, but her body was firmer now that she had joined a gym, a foolish luxury that he hadn't permitted while she lived with him.

She stared past him at his Jeep and said accusingly, "Where are the kids, Bradley? Why are you here without them? You said you'd be late dropping them off, and now you didn't even bring them?"

"They'll be here shortly," he lied. "I dropped them off for ice cream, that place just down the block. So we could have some time to talk."

Staring at him angrily, Jackie said, "They shouldn't have been left alone to go to the ice cream store! Where's your head at, Bradley? Go and get them right now!"

He said, "C'mon, let them grow up a little. They'll be okay. You can't baby them all the time, Jackie."

"I *don't* baby them. I just keep them safe," she snapped back at him. "You and I have absolutely nothing to *talk* about. Go get the kids and bring them here. I don't care if their cones are dripping all over you."

"Jackie...let me in, for god's sake! Let's not argue out here in the street!"

He looked around furtively.

She opened the door wider but didn't let her annoyance diminish in the least. "I'll give you five minutes to say whatever you have to say, then get out. And bring Peggy, Jimmy and Billy right back here where they belong. Or I'll go after them myself."

He stepped inside and shut the door, then bolted it, and Jackie was alarmed by that, so she said, "Don't bolt the door. I don't trust you."

"Relax, I'm harmless," he said.

He sat on the sofa while she folded her arms over her breasts and remained standing.

She said, "I don't know what your game is, but if you think you're going to sweet-talk me, you've got another think coming. Things have changed between us, Bradley. You're done bossing me around and putting bruises on me when you don't get your way."

In his most sincere tone, he said, "I'll never hurt you again, honey. I promise. You've made me see myself in a new light. I want you and me to get back together. It's the best thing for the kids. They need us to be a real family again. No matter what I did in the past, we now have to do what's best for our children."

"You should've been thinking that way during the whole time we were married."

"I told you, that's in the past! Give me a break! I promise you, I've changed!"

"It's too late. I'm not falling for your lies anymore. Besides, I'm seeing someone else."

Upon hearing that, Bradley got a vicious look on his face. He reached inside his jacket and clutched the handle of his knife. Malice oozed from his lips. "You're screwing some other *guy* with *my* kids in here? With their *bedrooms* right down the hall? They can probably hear him going at you hot and heavy—or is he some kind of *pansy?*"

"He's much *more* of a man than you'll ever be! And he doesn't need to beat up women to prove it!"

That was too much for Bradley. He jumped up, pulling out his knife. Jackie tried to run from him, but he grabbed her ponytail and pushed her down onto the sofa. Staring down at her, clutching her throat with the blade at her neck, he jeered at her, his spittle hitting her in her face.

"I tried to be *nice,* but you won't be nice to *me!* Big mistake, Jackie! Now you're gonna pay! You're *never* gonna see our kids again! You were a lousy wife and mommy anyway! You never turned me on! You acted like screwing me was a chore!"

Jackie managed to choke out a few words. "Please… don't kill me, Bradley…"

He laughed mockingly, then began stabbing her over and over after forcing a couch pillow over her face to muffle her screams.

He enjoyed every single stab.

When he finally stood up, he was breathing hard, sweating like mad, with blood spatter on his face. Then he looked down at her, and the couch pillow had fallen away and she stared up at him with wide-eyed sightless eyes and gaping bloody wounds.

He said, "Serves you right, you fucking bitch."

Then he pivoted and walked away to wash his hands and knife in her kitchen sink.

2

Behind Jackie's little house there was a carport where she kept her little gray Kia. The small backyard had a dilapidated six-foot-high unpainted board fence that looked old and ugly but made the yard safe from prying eyes.

Bradley stepped out of the back door, went to the car, and popped open the trunk using Jackie's key. Then he ducked back into the house, and when he let himself out again, he was carrying Jackie's bloody body wrapped up in a sheet. He went to the car once again and put her body in the trunk and closed it. Then he got into the driver's seat, started the engine, and backed out of the carport.

His plan was to bury Jackie's body somewhere where it wouldn't be found. Then he would ditch her car, maybe at the airport or perhaps in some patch of woods other than the place where he'd put her body. If her mother, father, or a friend of hers should get into her little house to check on her, the bloodstains would still be there to be discovered, but if he should be questioned about it, he'd feign ignorance. Meantime, he'd claim his three kids, who were now being watched over by his mother. The police would be reluctant to arrest him and take him away from his children without absolute proof that he was guilty of murder. They would see that the children were already overwhelmed with grief over their missing mother, and it would be far worse if they also lost their father.

Bradley drove away from Jackie's bungalow in her little gray Kia and passed through a succession of pleasant-looking suburban neighborhoods till he made it out of town and into the countryside on Pennsylvania Interstate 79. He spotted a shopping plaza with a Walmart and took that exit so he could buy a ten-by-ten tarp, a pick and a shovel. Then he got back on Route 79.

After driving about thirty or forty miles northward, he took another exit which put him on a two-lane blacktop that was sparsely populated, and he eventually pulled off the road and onto a rutted yellow-clay lane passing through a lonely-looking unplowed field bordered by woods and tall, thick weeds.

He warily looked all around as he bumped over the grassy field to the outskirts of the woods, then parked and shut the engine off.

It wasn't quite dark yet, and he wished that it was. But he had to do what he had to do because he felt it was too risky to drive around much longer with a dead body in the trunk. He figured it would grow darker as he dug the hole, and if somebody came up on him before he got started, he could say he was going to dig for earthworms to use them as bait.

He got out of Jackie's car, then pulled his knife out of a sheathe and made himself ready to stab somebody if he had to. So far, he saw nobody. So he took Jackie's bloody body out of the trunk, carried it to a patch of relatively clear ground, and grunted as he laid it down. Then he went back and got his brand-new shovel and pick from the trunk, returned to the body and started to dig.

"Hold it right there, mister! Where do you get off trying to bury somebody on *my* property?"

Bradley was so startled that he jumped back, and his eyes went wide. His heart leaped into his throat, and he almost dropped his shovel when he saw a double-barreled shotgun pointing directly at him. It was wielded by a person wearing a straw hat, a flannel shirt, baggy coveralls, and a bulky brown canvas jacket—clothing so gender nondescript that he couldn't be sure of the person's sex. Whether it was male or female, the voice that had stopped him dead in his tracks was uniquely rough and raspy, almost as if it belonged to a heavy smoker or to someone of either gender who was trying to sound utterly masculine.

Caught with the dead body of his murder victim, Bradley desperately raised his shovel in front of himself as if he wanted to swing it at the person suddenly confronting him.

The same gruff voice barked at him. "Drop the fucking shovel, asshole!"

He was scared enough to do so. Then he started stammering. "I-I-I didn't kill her. She died in her sleep, but I don't have the money for a funeral."

"Bullshit! You killed her!"

"I didn't!"

"You did. I don't want her buried here, though. I'll help you dispose of her properly."

Bradley could barely believe what he was hearing. Had he stumbled upon somebody like himself, in other words, a kindred spirit? Gathering his wits about him, he stammered, "Huh? You mean you'd help me?"

"For a price," the gruff voice answered.

In for a penny, in for a pound, Bradley thought, so he said, "How do I know I can trust you?"

"You gotta trust me, buster. You got no choice. Or else I'll shoot you and dispose of you both! Now, do as I say. Put her back in the trunk so we don't have to carry her any farther than necessary. I'll lead you across the field, and you follow me in your car."

"What should I call you?" Bradley asked, thinking that the name would reveal the sex.

"I'm called Sandy," came the reply, solving nothing, because it could be either male or female.

He/she led him toward a rickety farmhouse, then veered off toward a hog pen that stunk to high heaven. A dozen or more hogs were grunting and snorting in a filthy, muddy sty by an old, dilapidated barn.

Stopping where he was signaled to, Bradley got jolted by the sight of something that the hogs were tussling over when he suddenly thought it looked like a human hand and arm. He wanted to believe it was a figment of his addled imagination, but he was unable to fool himself into thinking that.

Sandy laughed at the look on Bradley's face. Motioning with her shotgun, she or he said, "Get out. Don't poke around. My hogs are hungry and they can sense they're gonna be fed."

When Bradley got out of the car, his nose wrinkled up, and he said, *"Peeyew!* What a *stink!"*

Sandy said, in his/her gruff unisex voice, "Don't *insult* my animals, buster! They're smarter than most people. But they get awful rotten mean if I don't feed 'em some-thin' they really *like* now and then. You did 'em an unwitting favor when you showed up here with food. Now open up that trunk and let's get to it!"

"You don't have to keep calling me Buster. My name's Bradley."

"I couldn't care less! Now let's get your wife outta the trunk. We can both do the lifting this time. But you better not try anything funny. I guarantee you I can dive for my shotgun in time to blow you away."

"Are you a woman or a man?" he finally asked.

"Sort of neither. But I'm mostly a she right now." The implications tumbled through Bradley's mind. He realized that Sandy might be a transsexual. He was taken aback by that thought, but he was willing to accept it. For now. He decided he didn't give a shit whether she was male, female or something in between. Good luck had come his way because she was helping him. It flickered through his mind that he might be able to kill her once her guard was down, so he could rob all the money and jewelry and stuff that might be in her farmhouse.

She leaned the shotgun against a fence post.

Bradley almost dove for a rock to hit her over her head. But instead he stammered, "I c-c-can't do it!"

"Can't do *what?* You turnin' chicken-shit on me?"

"I can't feed Jackie to those hogs. I can't stand the thought of them chewing on her, tearing her apart. Why can't I bury her like I planned to do?"

Sandy flared up and stared at him meanly, with her hands on her hips. "Because my hogs are *hungry*, that's why! A human body ain't good for nothin' when it's dead. Unless it donates organs or something. Well, in this case, the whole thing is being donated. I don't see what the big fuss is. It's a perfectly logical thing to do."

Bradley stared at her, struck speechless. He figured

she must be insane, which terrified him because he didn't yet know how deep her insanity went.

She said, "Now don't you poke around on me. Let's get her out of the trunk and give her the old heave-ho!"

They did exactly that. They tossed the corpse wrapped in the bloody sheet over the fence into the hog sty.

The hogs immediately started to go wild, pawing and pulling at the grisly bundle, tearing it apart and revealing parts of the bloody, mangled corpse.

Sandy chortled, but Bradley stepped back and started shaking, appalled and dismayed by what he had wrought.

He turned and started determinedly walking away from the ugly scene of hogs feasting on his own wife.

Sandy angrily called after him. "Hey! Where the hell do you think you're going?" She grabbed her shotgun and aimed it at his back.

He turned and faced her, putting his hands up as if they might ward off her kill shots.

Even more scared than before, he said, "N-n-nowhere. I'm not thinking straight. I'm all shook up. I know you're doing me a crazy kind of favor. Maybe you'll help me some more. Or at least let me go so I can do what I have to do."

Still covering him with the shotgun, she said, "What the *hell* are you *babbling* about?"

Trying his best to explain himself, he said, "My plan was to ditch this car and hitchhike back to my wife's place. I can't leave my Jeep there. I've got to get to it and drive it somewhere so it won't be there when her body is discovered and the cops come."

"Hitchhike?" Sandy said, looking somewhat perplexed. "You wanted to kill your wife, but why didn't you plan it out better?: You're an asshole when it comes to killing people, you know that?"

"So you have more experience than I do? You've fed other victims to your hogs?"

"Okay, so what? I admit it. So what're you gonna do about it? If you tell on me, I'll tell on *you*. Or I'll kill you right here and now. How do you like that?"

He realized that for the time being he was stuck with this crazy person, and hoping to make the best of it he said, "When we're done here, will you drive me to my Jeep so I can get it out of there?"

"I'll do that—but you'll owe me. What about your kids? Do you have any?"

"Three of them. But they're with my mom. If she never sees me again, she'll take over and raise them. I made her promise. My lease ran out, and I don't have anywhere to live. That's why I begged my wife to take me back—but she wouldn't listen."

"Hmph!" Sandy snorted. "Maybe she was smart. And maybe I'm nuts—but you can live with me. I need someone like you to help me with certain things. My pickup is over there at the other side of the barn. I'll drive you to wherever your Jeep is so we can start fixing your fuck-ups."

They climbed into her old battered pickup truck and Sandy turned the ignition and started driving down her long, rutted driveway. It was a forty-five-mile drive back to Jackie's house and Bradley worried the whole time, and ran at the mouth about it, too. Mostly he berated himself because he belatedly realized that his murder plan was stupid. Number one, he had left his Jeep in front of the house—why the hell didn't he at least put it in the carport after he pulled Jackie's Kia out? Or else he should've taken an Uber over there to confront her—

then if worse came to worse and he had to kill her, none of the neighbors would've seen his vehicle and made him a person of interest right away. Number two, he should've smothered her or choked her to death instead of using a knife; that way he could've left the place in pristine condition, not a bloody mess, and everybody, including the police, might have assumed that she had gone someplace where she wanted to go, instead of into a makeshift grave or, for that matter, into a sty full of hungry hogs.

He was greatly relieved when they got to within a block of Jackie's house and he spotted his Jeep still there. "Whew!" he said. "Maybe I'm almost home free!"

"That's if the police aren't inside laying for you," Sandy warned him.

"No, I don't think so," he said. "There's no crime scene tape."

"They're not dumb enough to leave it up if they're hiding in there, ready to put cuffs on you," Sandy said, sounding proud of her logical reasoning.

"Well, I've got to take that chance," Bradley said. "We didn't hear any murder reports on the truck radio on our way over here."

"Same thing," Sandy squelched. "The cops aren't dumb enough to call attention to themselves when they're laying a trap."

Bradley nervously thought about it as Sandy pulled in at the curb, behind his Jeep. Then he ventured to say, "Like I told you, I've got no choice. I've gotta get my Jeep out of here. Maybe I should even risk taking my time, going into the house for a while."

"Why the hell would you wanna do that?" said Sandy, sounding disgusted with him.

"I could maybe clean up the bloodstains real good,"

he said meekly. "Make it look like Jackie ran off some-where. I could say I brought the kids over but she wasn't home. Damn! I wish I would've choked her instead of stabbing her! Where the hell was my head at?"

"Well, I'm not waiting for you to go in and clean up," Sandy said adamantly. "I'm already taking a big chance, and you don't seem to appreciate it."

"No…no, I do," Bradley insisted half pleadingly. "I'll just jump in my Jeep and we'll go back to your farm. I'm assuming that's okay with you."

She didn't say it wasn't, so he did what he said he would do. He followed closely behind her pickup truck for thirty-some miles until she pulled into a convenience store with gas pumps out front. On the way to Jackie's house he had seen that her tank was three-quarters full, so when she pulled into a slot beside a pump he pulled in alongside her, wound down his window and shouted, "I didn't think you'd need gas. I don't, I'm half full."

She grimaced at him as if he were as clueless as a child and said irritably, "No, I don't need gas. But you do. Go in there and buy a big gasoline can, then come out here and fill it up."

It belatedly started to dawn on him what the gasoline was for, so he didn't ask any more questions. He just followed her instructions. After he was done with all that, they drove the final miles to her farm, and once again he followed her and she led him to where he had left Jackie's car, and he got out of his Jeep but she stayed behind the wheel of her pickup.

She stared at him, shaking her head at him, then said, "Get the gasoline out of your Jeep and get behind the wheel of the Kia and follow me. I'll take you to a perfect place."

He figured out what she meant, so he let himself be

led. After ten miles or so, she pulled her pickup off the blacktop and onto a rutted road through some woods, and then into a tight little inconspicuous clearing.

They got out of the vehicles and he stood there with his hands at his sides.

"Get the damn gasoline," she rasped at him. "Do I have to tell you what to do all the time? Or do you have a little bit of ability to think for yourself?"

Without sassing her, he got the big can of gasoline from the trunk of the Kia, and Sandy continued giving him orders. "Douse it good. Soak the front and back seats and the floorboards. I'll stuff a gas-soaked rag in the gas tank."

As he was doing the dousing, she tugged a large bandana from the hip pocket of her overalls and used it to sop up some gasoline from a puddle he had already made on the Kia's back seat. Then she uncaps the gas tank and stuffs the bandana like a fuse into the opening.

"Now light it and stand back," she said. "You have the matches I gave you."

He struck a match and lit the makeshift fuse, and the car went up in flames.

Bradley and Sandy backed away, watching the gigantic ball of fire.

Bradley wanted to give her a high-five, but he thought maybe he shouldn't.

3

When Detectives Vince Spivak and Jerry Delaney arrived at the murder scene, crime scene tape was strung around the perimeter and two patrolmen were in the front yard, by the porch. Spivak parked his unmarked black Impala at the curb behind a black-and-white patrol car and he and Delaney both got out. They were each in their late thirties, wearing dark suits with starched white shirts and striped ties, and they had an athletic look about them even though they both were fifteen to twenty pounds overweight. Spivak's reddish hair was going grayer than Delaney's light brown but wasn't receding quite as much. As they looked toward the house where they knew that something very bad awaited them, they shook their heads and scowled at one another. Just then, because their gold badges were in plain sight, worn on thongs around their necks, an elderly woman jumped out of the back seat of the parked patrol car and blurted, "Please…are you the detectives? My daughter lives here with my grandchildren. I'm Edna Bracken. I need to know what's going on."

"We don't know much yet," Spivak said. "We're just arriving."

Of course he and Delaney knew that there likely had been a homicide, but they didn't want to say that yet. The victim hadn't conclusively been identified, so it might turn out that she wasn't the woman's daughter; at least there was a slim chance of that. And, for that matter, thus far, there had not been any mention of dead or missing children.

"Please don't tell me you're homicide detectives," Edna Bracken said. "I'm Jackie's mom. This is my daughter's apartment, and nobody is telling me anything."

Delaney said, "It's best if you just let us go in and do our job, Mrs. Bracken. Please stay out here. Sit in the patrol car. We'll want to talk with you shortly when we learn more."

Trembling and crying, she backed away as the two detectives moved past her. They walked up to the patrolmen and the older-looking one said, "The next-door neighbor was trying to do a welfare check, and she looked through a front window and thought she saw blood on part of the living room couch. That's all she could see, but she called 9-1-1. She was babbling at us when we got here. We told her to go home and call somebody to stay with her. She's in shock, and who can blame her? But she made the mistake of phoning the dead woman's mother and now we have her to deal with, as you've already learned. Sorry for the surprise."

"We'll deal with it the best we can," Spivak said.

The younger-looking patrolman said, "It's a bloody mess in there. Worst I've ever seen."

He didn't look old enough to have seen much up until now, but the detectives let it slide.

The older patrolman said, "There's no body in the

house, just a whole lot of blood on the floor, the furniture, the walls and ceiling. That's why we called it in as a homicide."

"You shouldn't have jumped to that conclusion just yet," Spivak said. "The victim might still be alive. Maybe kidnapped. Let's hope that's the case."

The older patrolman said, "By the looks of what's inside here, Mrs. Bracken's daughter must be dead, and maybe her grandchildren too. I hope not. I hope they're with somebody close to them, maybe a relative who's keeping them safe."

The two detectives nodded an amen to that, then donned latex gloves and entered the apartment. The first thing they saw was the blood-soaked couch and pillow, the blood puddles on the carpet, and the blood splatter on the walls. They stared at it for a while, taking it all in, hoping for clues and not immediately spotting any.

Delaney said, "This sure looks like overkill, Vince."

"Yeah, no attempt to make it look like a burglary gone wrong," Spivak agreed. "The flat-screen TV and the computer are still here. Whoever did this was carrying a lot of rage. Likely somebody real close to her. Which ought to give us some kind of handle on who we need to home in on."

"Husband, ex-husband or boyfriend," Spivak conjectured. "How usual."

"Let's hope it turns out that way," said Delaney. "I hate whodunnits. But if it turns out to be an ex-husband, it's gonna be bad for the kids."

"Assuming they're still alive and well," said Spivak.

———

SANDY HELD the farmhouse door open and Bradley Kelter stepped around her to enter her living room. He remained standing as she took off her heavy coat and plopped down onto a worn-out couch. His nose started to run because of the mustiness and the dust. Looking down at his feet, he saw that the darkly flower-patterned carpet was threadbare. Apparently Sandy wasn't a good housekeeper and wasn't swimming in money.

She said, "*Whew!* I'm pooped!"

He stared at her. Now that her coat was off, he was pretty sure she had breasts. Or was it just that she had a man's well-developed pectorals? It bothered him that he still didn't quite know how to peg her in terms of gender.

"I hope you appreciate what I'm doing for you," she said, eyeing him piercingly.

Bradley couldn't help blurting, "Are you a man or a woman? Forgive me for asking, but I honestly can't tell."

"Why is it important to you?"

"I don't know."

"Are you going to hit on me if I'm a girl?" she said in a mischievously threatening way.

"I don't think so. No," Bradley asserted.

She took her straw hat off and let her hair fall. It was brown with streaks of gray. She said, "My whole life my brain has told me that I'm female, but somehow I was born with the wrong organs. Sit down. Make yourself comfortable, and I'll tell you about it."

He wondered if he really wanted to know whatever she had to say.

———

DETECTIVES Spivak and Delaney were still at the crime scene, standing in the middle of the bloody living room, and Spivak said, "Nothing more we can do here. We've got a BOLO out on Jackie's car. When we find it, we'll probably find her body. And it might give up some clues."

"Let's hope," Delaney said doubtfully. "Meanwhile, where the hell are her three kids? If we find them, we probably find her estranged husband. I hope he didn't kill *them*. But Jackie's mother is sure he's who we have to be looking for. There's no love lost between the two of them."

"But we can't jump the gun on this, Jerry. He may be innocent in spite of her dislike for him. We've got to find him. I put a BOLO out on his Jeep as well as Jackie's car. We find the Jeep, we find *him*—and hopefully the kids are safe and sound. Too bad we couldn't reach his mother or sister. That's where they might be. I'd like to give Jackie's mother some hope."

"Let's get out of here and start canvassing the neighbors. Maybe somebody saw or heard something."

"We've got to talk to the mother some more," Spivak said.

"Not right now," said Delaney. "She's too distraught. We can't let her come in here either."

"Maybe tomorrow or the next day, after it's cleaned up," Spivak said. "She can tell us if she notices anything missing."

They exited the apartment, and Mrs. Bracken got out of the patrol car and hurried up to them while they were still on the porch. Excited even through her grief, she said, "Bradley's mother just called me on my cell phone! Thank God—she has my grandchildren! That bastard dropped them off with her! She's a good woman. God only knows where *he* is! I'm more sure than ever that he must've killed my daughter! He probably wanted them out of the way first."

———

Lying flat on her back on the couch with her right hand over her eyes, Sandy said, "I don't value human life very much, Bradley. You should keep that in mind if you ever try to cross me. My feeling is that the only thing wrong with planet Earth is the people on it. We exploit and kill every other life form, put it in zoos, or cause it to go extinct. If not for us, all the other animals, even the dodo birds that were clubbed to death by vicious, ignorant sailors back in the 1800s, would still be here."

Bradley ventured to say, "You sound like an educated...uh...person."

"What do you mean—*person?*" she snapped back at him. "I'm a *woman*, and don't you forget it! My cock and balls are gonna go bye-bye."

Bradley was immediately stunned and perplexed. In awe, he said, "You're gonna be a transvestite?"

"No, stupid! A transvestite is a halfway kind of thing —a transition. I'm going all the way. I'm going to be what's called a transsexual—but I hate that word! I'm going to be the *woman* I was always meant to *be*."

"But you acted like a man for your whole life?"

"As much of a man as you are, or probably more so. I was in the Marine Corps, I jumped out of planes. I did two tours in Afghanistan, got a Purple Heart, a Bronze Star, and an honorable discharge. Sandy Jacobs, male war hero! I killed people over there, and some of them didn't deserve it. Like the war prisoners I shot. When I came back home, I made up my mind to only kill the ones who need to die."

"What do you mean, *need to?*"

"The ones who cross me. Or the ones I can take their money from or keep on cashing their social security checks. I shoot them or strangle them, then chop them up and feed them to my hogs."

Somewhat aghast at this, Bradley said, "Why didn't we chop Jackie up, then?"

"I didn't want to take the time while I still had to keep the shotgun on you. But they won't eat all of her. There will be stuff left. *Incriminating* stuff—and we'll have to rake it all up and bury what's left of her or burn it in a real hot fire, down to tiny bone fragments and ashes in a pit or a barrel. But we have to make sure there aren't any of her teeth left or bones with the marrow intact because that can yield DNA."

Bradley thought about that, then said, "You've got it all figured out, haven't you? I've got to say, what I did was a straight murder, not all that grisly, in a way. Not like feeding people to a bunch of hungry hogs."

"Come off it! You're no Goody Two-Shoes! I saw her wounds. You butchered the hell out of her. Stabbed her and sliced her more times than you could count."

"Maybe I did. I don't remember. But I got no pleasure from feeding her to your hogs. I don't have the stomach for that."

"You'll get used to it, maybe even come to enjoy it," Sandy told him.

He said, "I have to admit I kind of admire you for it. Being so practical about it, I mean. No body, no crime. It's the best way not to risk getting caught."

"Good, because I can use your help. I've got two

people in mind that I can rob and kill, but it'll go easier and be less risky if I go in with a partner."

"Hey, I'm game. I'm gonna need some way to get money to live on. I can't collect on my wife's insurance policy because I'm sure the police will think I'm their prime suspect."

"They won't think, they'll *know*. Because you weren't clever enough. But now you've got me to lean on. I'll be the brains and you'll be my accomplice."

"In other words, a flunky," Bradley said sullenly. "I'm not sure I like that, Sandy."

"Suck it up if you know what's good for you," she warned him.

———

IT WAS DARK OUT NOW, and Detectives Spivak and Delaney could glimpse streetlamps and neon-lit street-level stores through the coffee shop windows as they sat in a red leatherette booth with pastries and large cups of coffee in front of them. Jerry was glum, and Vince didn't try to butt into his glumness because he knew that family-type crimes always made Jerry go into the dumps thinking about his wife, Jenny, and his kids, Billy and Janie, ages eight and ten. Vince wasn't married and had no children, but in a way that didn't make much difference in how he felt.

All cops were tasked with having to bear up under the depressing first-hand knowledge of the horrors that human beings were capable of.

Finally breaking the silence, Spivak said, "Why is it that neighbors almost never hear anything when a murder goes down?"

"Because the murderers try real hard *not* to be heard," Delaney answered.

"I think people try real hard not to hear *anything*," Spivak said. "If they *do* hear anything they block it out because they don't want to be involved. All we did was wear out shoe leather. And time. According to protocol, we should've spoken to Kelter's mother and sister right away, in person. At least we got the bastard's mother on the phone and confirmed that she has the children. I don't think she knows much more. But we're sitting here waiting to see his sister on *her* schedule. What's her name? Melissa?"

"Melissa Kelter. Unmarried. I don't think she's sandbagging us," Delaney said. "When I got her on her cell phone, she said that she was in a late meeting with a client of some type and she didn't think he should be present while she meets with *us*. I don't blame her for that."

Spivak said, "Well, let's finish snacking, which I could've done without. Talk about wasting time. We'd better be on our way. I just want to get moving so I can feel like I'm doing something. She said she'd meet us at her office at nine o'clock, right?"

"Yeah, she's an accountant of some sort," Delaney said, "But if we head over there right now we'll be too early. Might as well finish our coffee first. We've got at least twenty minutes to kill."

In the car on their way to meet Melissa Kelter, Spivak said, "I wonder how much in denial she's going to be about her brother. It's hard for folks to admit one of their siblings might be a murderer, so they erect mental barriers. The obvious facts don't matter to them. They become delusional, they can't stand the shame of having a killer in their family."

"We shouldn't even tell her he's our top suspect," Delaney said. "Let her draw her own conclusions. After all, we don't have hard proof against him just yet."

"Yeah, but the circumstantial evidence has been building up from the start. Like, why didn't he bring the three children to Jackie like he was supposed to? It seems obvious that he knew what he was going to do to her and didn't want them to see their mother being butchered. He probably didn't want to have to kill *them*. Which he would've had to do if they saw him do it. He couldn't leave them as witnesses."

"I think you're right, Jerry. We don't tell the sister that Bradley's a suspect or even a person of interest, we just say we're trying to find him in case he's a victim, just like Jackie. That way she'll probably open up about his background. What he was like growing up, what were his goals in life, what underlying tendencies did he have, and so on. Maybe he picked on Melissa or hurt her in the same ways that he hurt Jackie, according to what Jackie's mother told us about. Most abusers start early, foisting their aggression on women who are close at hand."

Delaney said, "It's been over eighteen hours since we got on the case, and it feels like we've been swimming through Jell-O. I already phoned my wife to tell her we're on a case, and I talked to the kids and they're okay, but stuff like this still makes me worry too much. I want to run home and hug them for a long time."

"We haven't exactly been standing still, Vince. We've filled in a lot of background on Bradley and Jackie Kelter, thanks to his mother-in-law. I don't think she was exaggerating. He was definitely an abuser. When he beat up on Jackie he made her wear long sleeves to cover it up. That time she went to the hospital with a broken wrist, she kept on denying the abuse and refusing to prosecute

—till she finally moved out on him and got a restraining order."

"Restraining orders are a hazard in and of themselves," Spivak said. "We both know that it's often the final straw for wife beaters. It enrages them enough to move on to the next level."

"We have to arrest Bradley Kelter before he decides to act out even worse. I have a hunch he might hurt more women if we don't stop him. He unleashed an insane rage on Jackie. He probably stabbed her multiple times and got off on it, or she wouldn't have bled out so much. I think he's a serial killer in the making."

———

AT SUNUP THE NEXT MORNING, the hogs were busy eating something down at the far end of the hog pen when Bradley Kelter opened the gate, wheeled out a wheelbarrow from inside the chain-link fence, then shut and secured the gate again.

He started pushing the wheelbarrow across the field. He had a nauseated look on his face because he was wheeling his wife's mangled and devoured body parts, along with the ripped-up, dirty, and bloody sheet that she was formerly wrapped in. Some of her heavier bones, along with her skull, had patches of skin still on them.

Bradley wheeled his gruesome load out to where Sandy was digging a shallow hole in the ground, about forty feet from the sty. He looked at the big can of gasoline near where she was digging, and she stopped and leaned the shovel she had been using, which was the one he had bought yesterday, against a tree.

"I hope you collected it all," she said, peering at the meager contents of the wheelbarrow.

"I did like you said. I dumped the raw meat and hog feed down at one end of the pen to make them go there, then I scooped up everything I could."

"Well, dump all of it in the hole. It's gonna be our burn pit."

He dumped the grisly stuff into the hole, then pulled the wheelbarrow back a piece.

"Now pour the gas," said Sandy.

He picked up the heavy five-gallon can and poured lots of gasoline into the hole over the ugly little load that he had collected. He tamped it all down so that nothing stuck out. Then he stepped back and thought about what he had done, surprising himself that he felt no remorse, only a desire and a hope that he would get away with it.

Sandy stuck a match and tossed it, jumping back because the blaze was instantaneous and huge.

4

Melissa Kelter's accounting office was in a two-story store-front on Plum Street in Elizabeth, Pennsylvania, twelve miles from Pittsburgh off Route 51 South. It was between a pizza shop and a bistro called the Red Lion, and Jerry Delaney was familiar with the location.

"They have bands performing from six to nine on Thursdays in the summertime, from June to August, right outdoors here," Delaney informed Spivak. "Each band is sponsored by a merchant or a corporation. It's a really nice thing. They close off the square and put up a bandstand at the far end, and a few hundred people show up every time unless it rains. They sit on chairs and tables that the community provides, and a lot of them bring their own folding chairs, and they eat and drink and enjoy the music, and some of them get up and dance because there's always a space for it, right in front of the bandstand."

"That sounds like something I'd like," said Spivak. "Why didn't you tell me about it?"

"I did, just now."

"Thanks—now that it's September. Any chance they'd extend the band season?"

"No, it's over. I never mentioned it 'cause I didn't think it was your kind of thing."

"It would've been if they were having a good jazz band once in a while."

"It's mostly country and rock and roll. Pull into that lot across from the bank."

"It says PNC customers only."

"But the branch is closed, and the lot is empty."

"Oh…okay."

Spivak parked, and they got out and walked to Plum Street which was in the next block.

MELISSA KELTER, CPA, was printed in gold letters on a glass door. The place looked mostly dark, except there was a glow of light from an office deep inside. Jerry Delaney tried the door, and it opened and he and Vince went in after the door chimed. A female voice called out to them, "Come on back, I've been waiting for you for a while."

They entered a neat, businesslike office with pastoral paintings on the walls, and Melissa was sitting behind her large desk with a computer and keyboard to her right.

"You said nine o'clock," Spivak told her. "Or we would've come earlier."

"Well, I came earlier than I thought because I couldn't stand the suspense," she said. "I don't like being Bradley's sister, but I do want to help you if I can."

The detectives sat in folding chairs in front of her desk, and she sat back down. They took note of the fact that she was quite attractive, probably in her late twenties. She wore tight-fitting jeans and a Metallica T-shirt.

Her ash-blonde hair was pulled back into a ponytail, and her eyeglasses were dashingly fashionable light-gray frames.

"I'm Detective Spivak. We talked on the phone," Spivak said. "We're from the county sheriff's office. This is my partner, Detective Delaney. Obviously, we need to talk with you about your brother."

"Well, have a seat. There's no doubt in my mind that he murdered Jackie. I've always known that he's capable of the worst things that anyone can imagine. So nothing about him surprises me."

Delaney said, "We'd like you to tell us more about him than what we already know. We pulled his rap sheet and there are some incidents that are disturbing. He never did any jail time, but there were a few things that his lawyer was able to bargain down to minor charges and short probations."

Melissa took a deep breath and let it out, then said, "The system enabled him, just like my mother did. If she'd been harder on him, she may have straightened him out before he got worse. He did things to me that he should've been punished for."

"Abusive things?" Spivak ventured to ask, "I'm sorry if you don't like talking about it, but we need to know."

She stared into space, looking grim, then faced Spivak and Delaney and said, "He started acting out against me and kept it up from when he was little, maybe about eight. I'm three years younger than he is. He would steal things and blame it on me, and I'd get punished because my parents doted on him and thought he could do no wrong. He had an uncanny way of setting me up, even when we were young. He'd steal money and cigarettes and stuff. Then he'd gloat when I got spanked."

"At *three,* he made you get blamed for stealing ciga-rettes?" Delaney said with surprise.

"Well, no, that came later," Melissa explained. "But his torments run together in my mind like a waking nightmare."

"Sorry to hear that," Delaney offered. "I mean that sincerely, Melissa. Vince and I both care deeply about what the bad guys' victims have to go through. We understand how badly the survivors suffer, and it really gets to us. It's one of the main reasons we keep doing our job."

"Well, I want to help put him away where he belongs, so I'll tell you some things I've never been able to tell anyone else, and it's not easy for me to do that." She steeled herself, then opened up, in a near whisper, without making eye contact. "One time when I was nine years old, I was washing dishes, and he sneaked up behind me and kicked me between my legs, right on my…my pelvic bone…and I fell down screaming. He ran out of the kitchen laughing. Then he told my mom he wasn't even there when it happened, and as usual, he made her believe him. She asked me if I saw him kick me, and I admitted that I didn't because he was behind me, and she took that as an exoneration. He was as sly as a snake. He always could get away with things, just like the punks who work the justice system to their advan-tage day in and day out."

"Nobody knows that better than we do," Delaney said grimly.

"Amen," Spivak acknowledged.

"My brother actually made the football team in the eleventh grade," Melissa said. "And for a while, he seemed almost normal. Jackie was a cheerleader, and that's when she started dating him. He even stopped picking on me for a while, but it didn't last. Then he got married and moved out. A blessed relief. I hated him so much that my hatred influenced my career choices. I have a degree in accounting but I don't plan for it to be my future. I have a lot of respect for what you do in law enforcement. I hope to get into the FBI. I'm taking night courses in criminology and criminal justice."

"What we do is a tough gig," Spivak warned her.

She blinked and said, "I know, but I'm up for it. Wanting to see guys like my brother get their comeuppance undoubtedly motivated me in that direction. I was scared to death of him. The house I grew up in didn't seem like a home at times. It was more like a torture chamber, thanks to him. I had to get out of there, which is why I didn't want to go to Pitt. I wanted to enroll at an out-of-town university, so that's what I did. I had an academic scholarship that gave me my choice of any place that would accept me. I chose WVU. That's where I did my graduate and undergraduate work."

"We think your brother is on the lam," Spivak said. "There's a huge amount of blood at Jackie's apartment, but no body. But so much blood would indicate that she probably didn't survive. We don't think Bradley was another victim. We suspect that he was the perpetrator."

Melissa said, "I know he was beating Jackie up because she told me about it before she filed a restraining order, which I encouraged her to do. She was a sweet person, and my brother didn't deserve or appreciate her. He doesn't deserve *anybody*. And if he killed her, I hope he gets what he deserves—which is the death penalty."

"I can't argue with that," said Spivak.

"Quite a few murder cases would go unsolved if we couldn't use the death penalty as a bargaining chip,"

Delaney said. "People who say it's not a deterrent don't know what they're talking about. These creeps like making *other* people die but *they* always want to opt out."

"I agree," said Melissa. "I research cases, and I know what you're talking about."

"Do you have any idea where your brother might have run to?" Spivak asked.

"If I did, I'd tell you. I hope he kills himself before he harms anybody else. I'm sorry if that sounds cruel, but I can't help feeling that way. If he goes to prison, I'll apply for custody of the children. I'd hate to see them go into foster care, and Jackie's mom is too old to keep them."

"I'm glad to hear you're willing to do that," Spivak said.

"Well, I wouldn't trust my mother to raise them either, not after the way she raised me and Bradley. She's a widow who can barely take care of herself."

Delaney and Spivak nodded sympathetically. Then Delaney said, "I hope you realize your goal of getting into the FBI is going to be a tough row to hoe if you have to do it with two kids to raise, but you seem to be the kind of person who could make it work."

"I hope you're right," Melissa said.

The detectives stood up to go and got her assurance that they were welcome to get back in touch with her if more questions should arise.

Later, in the car, Jerry said, "Her brother kicked her in her vagina when he was only twelve years old. If that's not evidence of a hatred of women festering in him at a tender age, I don't know what is. Sometimes it seems like certain people's lives don't really matter very much, except in the worst way. They fuck up everything they can, and then they move on. Is that the way it's supposed to be? Us against them?"

"Damn, for a guy who's got a wife and two kids, you're one hell of a cynic," Vince Spivak said.

"Yeah, well, I saw the way you looked at Melissa like she makes you want to get encumbered. Maybe you should ask her out."

"She's probably at least fifteen years younger than me."

"See? You already did the math. Don't let the age difference stop you."

5

As Sandy and Bradley were driving after dark in her pickup, she filled him in on how the job would go down. He listened intently, amazed at how fast his criminal career was unfolding.

"We're going to the house where Ed and Mary Warner live," she told him.

He has a rare coin collection that we can sell for a lot of loot, and I have a guy who will fence them and keep his mouth shut. I used to clean the Warners' house for them, and the wife always stood over me as if it had to be fucking *perfect!* I always kept a pleasant smile on my face, even though I hated their guts. I had to make them trust me."

Bradley chuckled. "You're a sly one, Sandy. Again, I admire that. What's gonna be my share of the take?"

"I don't know, I'll make my mind up after I see how well you perform. You better not panic on me. If you do, I'll leave three corpses instead of two."

"Aren't we gonna feed them to your hogs?"

"Don't be stupid. There's no need to haul around two

dead bodies in the bed of my pickup truck—although I've done that a couple of other times. I chuckled to myself and called it bringing home the groceries."

"Groceries?"

"For my hogs. They're groceries for my hogs. That's how I think of 'em sometimes. Might as well get some humor out of it."

He made a little huffing sound, a ghost of a laugh because he was so nervous. He patted the pistol under his belt. It was a pistol with a silencer that she had armed him with for tonight's gig. He said, "I've never done this exact kind of thing before, but I'm psyched up. In fact, I have a hard-on. Is that pretty strange?"

"Yeah," she said. "But you're a strange dude."

She pulled the truck into the Warners' driveway, then parked and shut off the engine.

Before they get out, she let Bradley in on some more of her plan.

"Follow me and stay close behind me," she said. "The living room and kitchen lights are on, which means they're home. I'm gonna go up and knock, and when they see it's me, they won't even hesitate, they'll open the door to let me in. Duck back to one side so they won't see you till you shove them back with your gun in their faces."

She led the way up onto the porch and knocked. Nothing happened, so she knocked again. Then Ed Warner came to the door and opened it with a smile, saying, "Well, hi, Sandy! What a pleasant surprise! Will you have some cookies and hot chocolate with us?"

Looking past Sandy, Bradley saw that Mr. Warner was an affable middle-aged guy with a pot belly and a thick mop of gray hair.

Suddenly turning more mean than Bradley had ever

seen her, Sandy barked, "Fuck you and your hot choco-late, you old piece of shit!"

She shoved him backward and he thudded onto the floor.

Mary Warner jumped up from the sofa, dropping her crocheting needles and whatever she was working on.

Bradley came in, pointing his gun and silencer at her, and Sandy pulled a knife—the same one Bradley had used to kill his wife. She jeered at Mary Warner, soft and plump in a billowing old house dress.

"Were you crocheting again, you fucked up old biddy? Another doily? Number one thousand or so? You kept giving them to me, and I kept throwing the goddamn things in my compost pile!"

Ed Warner started pulling himself to his feet, and Sandy allowed him to get up off of the floor. To Bradley, she said, "Give me the gun now, and you take back your knife."

They quickly exchanged weapons.

"Please don't hurt us," the old man pleaded. "We were good to you, Sandy. What do you want?"

"Your fucking coin collection, that's what. I know where the safe is, and you're gonna open it."

"I'll do anything you want. Just don't hurt us."

But apparently Mary knew they were doomed, and she started crying hysterically.

"Oh, Ed, don't you get it?" she wailed. "They're going to have to kill us because we *know* Sandy! She's not even trying to disguise herself!"

She kept on bawling.

Sandy said, "Shut her up, Bradley! Hit her over the head with something before someone hears her and calls the cops."

He picked up a heavy statuette and cracked her head

with it, and she sagged and collapsed onto the couch as the figurine fell and shattered.

Her husband cried out, "Mary! *Mary!* Oh, God, you hit her hard enough to kill her!"

Sandy shouted, "Shut the fuck up, you old coot! Or I'll start cutting you! Which I'm going to do anyway if you don't tell us the combination."

She stomped to a closet and flung open the door to reveal that it was filled with winter coats and such, but when she pulled the coats down, hangers and all, a hidden safe was revealed.

Ed was still wailing. "*Please!* Let me call an ambulance for Mary!"

Sandy said, "Don't you get it, Ed? She's not gonna *need* an ambulance ever again! And we're gonna start slicing off your toes and fingers one at a time if you don't open this safe! Now, do you want to die a quick death or a slow, painful one?"

With tears streaming down his cheeks, Ed Warner shakily staggered over to the safe in the closet, kneeled down, and started working the combination.

When the door to the safe swung open, Sandy immediately shot him in the back of his head. He dropped to the floor, flat on his stomach, gushing blood. Sandy watched as he kicked, thrashed, and died. Then she turned toward Bradley and said, "You know what to do. Kill her."

Bradley got an evil grin on his face—then he started stabbing—and he stabbed over and over, just as he did with his wife. He couldn't control himself. His pent-up rage overcame him.

Sandy watched him stabbing, a slight smile on her face. But finally she spoke up.

"Okay, Bradley, you've had enough enjoyment. We

have to cut it short—no pun intended. Go into the powder room and clean yourself up while I get the goodies out of the safe. I don't want you getting blood drops on my truck seat."

Bradley went into the powder room with the bloody knife.

Sandy dragged Ed's body away from the closet and the safe. Then she knelt and poked around inside till she pulled out a steel box. She opened it and saw that it was filled with sheets of mounted vintage coins.

Bradley came out of the powder room looking less bloody and disheveled, and his face and hair were wet. "Is that what we came for?" he asked with a smile.

"Damn straight," Sandy said. "I told you so. Now let's get the hell out of here!"

6

In her upstairs bedroom at the farmhouse, Sandy was undressing. In contrast to the funky, dirty, un-dusted, un-vacuumed Salvation Army decor of the downstairs, her bedroom was a distinctly feminine reflection of the kind of woman she wished to be.

She watched herself in a full-sized mirror.

She had allowed Bradley to stand in the doorway and watch, and he was in awe. First she took off her straw hat, letting her wavy shoulder-length hair tumble down. Then she shed her cumbersome, figure-hiding clothes— the flannel shirt, bibbed coveralls, and clodhoppers he was used to seeing her in.

When she took off her bra, he saw that it had padding in it that had made her breasts look larger, even when they were under the bibbed part of her coveralls, but actually they were the budding kind of breasts that might belong to a prepubescent girl.

To Bradley's surprise, she had a nice, trim body with long, lithe musculature. But she had turned away from him so he couldn't see her genitals.

She turned and came toward him, and he stopped himself from looking downward because he didn't want to incur her wrath. Focusing on her face and upper body, he couldn't believe how sensuous she looked. And the utter strangeness of it all definitely turned him on.

Sandy laughed coquettishly and knowingly.

She said, "Do you find me alluring? I swear, your tongue is hanging out. Tell me the truth, Bradley. I think you want to fuck me."

She put her arms around him and pulled him tight.

"Do you still...uh..."

"Yes, I still have them. But now that we'll soon have the money from the coin collection, I'll be making an appointment with the surgeon. I've been taking estrogen and other substances, and they're working. I feel more womanly than ever."

"You *look* womanly," he said. "Totally womanly." *If I don't look down*, he thought to himself.

He wanted to put his hands on her breasts. They looked like his sisters did when he used to spy on her when he was a teenager.

She kissed him deeply...then pulled back...and said softly, "Would you like to go to bed with me? There are things I can do for you. And after my operation, I'll be able to do more."

She kissed him again, and he gave himself over to her without reservation.

7

F our days after the start of the Jackie Kelter investigation, Spivak and Delaney admitted despairingly to one another that, in spite of all their hard work, they were spinning their wheels. They didn't know what to do next because they had run out of leads. Spivak suggested that they take a break by seven o'clock on a Friday in August because they badly needed to get a few hours of uninterrupted rest and hopefully reinvigorate themselves at least a little bit. It had been their experience that with a much-needed break, some new perspectives might dawn on them, and maybe that would happen this time as well. "Or else a tip might come in," Delaney said. "A viable tip, not more crank calls. That's clearly what we need."

But Vince didn't tell his buddy Jerry Delaney that he wasn't going to hit the sack. Instead, he was going to phone Melissa Kelter and ask her to dinner. When he worked up the courage to do so, he felt good that she not only recognized his voice right away but also remembered his first and last names. But then he realized that maybe she had the card he had given her right in front of her.

She said, "I already ate a big Panera roast beef and guacamole sandwich right here at my desk while I was going through some files, but I could go for a glass of wine or two, if you don't mind."

"That's fine," he said. Then added, "I mostly just want to see you."

"I hope it's not just to pick my brain some more," she said mildly.

"No," he said. "I need a rest from all that. I can pick you up at your office, or we can meet wherever you say."

"Do you know the Elbow Room?"

He said that he did, and they agreed to meet there. He got there first, asked for a table, and ordered a beer, and felt a little bit like a teenager on his first date. He ran the age difference through his head again and decided to throw caution to the wind in that regard. He found himself being glad to know she wasn't married, but he warned himself to slow down because he knew next to nothing about her on a personal level, and perhaps he never would. Nothing serious might ever develop between them, and it certainly wouldn't if he got too pushy.

He kept watching the door and sipping his beer till it was almost gone, and finally, he was relieved to see her come in. She was wearing tight jeans again with a Metallica T-shirt, but it wasn't the same one, although it was just as flashy. He decided it was probably her way of not always wanting to appear prim and businesslike. She smiled and came over to him, and he stood and pulled out her chair.

"Ah, you're a gentleman of the old school," she commented.

Which made him once again think of their age difference.

But then she said, "Good manners are refreshing. I haven't dated too much lately because most of the younger guys are clods. They pick up a couple of tabs when they go out with someone. Then they expect to get laid."

He had mixed feelings about the frankness younger people exhibited about matters of sex. He would've thought that the torment her brother had wreaked on her might have made her wary or perhaps even frigid, and he was relieved that it apparently had not. She appeared more vivacious than she had been during the interview in her office, which made her even more desirable in Vince's eyes.

The waiter came over, and he ordered another beer after she asked for a glass of Chablis.

She sipped and smiled. "Just as good as I remembered," she quipped. "They don't water it down." She eyed him and said, "Did you eat yet? Maybe I could just pick at something if you want to order."

"Want some chicken wings?"

"They have really good ones here. I guess I could eat onc or two."

"I'll order six with an order of fries."

He signaled the waiter, who came over promptly, wrote the order down, and headed toward the kitchen ordering slot to the left of the bar.

"This is nice," Melissa said. "I don't get out enough."

"Let's do it again, then," he ventured to say.

She asked, "Are you married?"

He said, "No. Never have been."

She said, "Neither have I."

"I know," he informed her. "We Googled you before we interviewed you. Standard practice."

"I should've known," she said. "In any event, I never got up the nerve to plunge into marrying somebody. Most marriages end in divorce, but I don't think that's what stopped me."

He wondered if her reluctance had something to do with her brother having shown her the worst side of manhood, but he didn't say so. Instead, he turned the conversation toward himself. "I've had two long-term relationships," he admitted. "But after a while, both women came to realize they didn't want to be married to a cop. Sometimes I think they probably made the right choice."

"That might be true," Melissa said. "But on the other hand, maybe if both halves of a couple are in law enforcement, they'll understand each other well enough to stick it out."

"I don't know about that," he said. "Maybe all the rough spots would blend together from both of their perspectives and make things worse."

"Oh, you sound like such an optimist," she said. "But you surely know how cruel people can be to each other, and so do I."

"You're talking about your brother?"

"What else?" she said grimly.

He could see how hurt she still was by what had been done to her back when she was a vulnerable little girl. And he hoped he wasn't going to find out that the damage was permanent.

In a little while, his order came, and they ordered two more drinks to wash down the wings and fries.

8

J erry Delaney slept fitfully Friday night, then got up early on Saturday morning and made some repairs around the house, then took his wife and kids to a neighborhood playground. He tossed a baseball back and forth with Billy and Janie after watching them having fun on the monkey bars, the seesaw, and the basketball court.

Spending time with his family in the midst of a homicide investigation—he might as well call it that because he truly felt that Jackie Kelter must be dead—always made him feel a little schizophrenic as if he didn't totally deserve this kind of happiness, and so something beyond his power was destined to come along and make it end.

His wife Jenny, on the other hand, seemed to bask in these brief interludes of normalcy even though she wasn't really cut out to be a cop's wife. She thought it was more dangerous than it actually was. Jerry had told her often that statistically, very few law officers gave their lives in the line of duty. But they both knew that when it happened, God forbid, their wives and kids were crushed and devastated in more ways than one. Jenny had been to two funerals for men in blue, and she never wanted to hear bagpipes ever again.

She had gone to the ladies' room a short while ago, and now she came back and sat with him on a bench. Voicing his previous thoughts, he told her, "Sometimes it's hard to keep things in perspective when I'm looking at photos of murder victims one day, and the next day I'm looking at my kids playing in a park."

He knew she liked to hear talk like that, which gave her hope that he might change jobs. She even pressed it a little bit, saying, "That's why I think you should move on, try to do something else, even if it doesn't pay as much. I'm willing to help out by getting a side job."

"I know you are, honey. But you're already working full-time as a wife and mom, and I know it's not easy. I'm not one of these guys who think it's a big nothing. I don't put you down for not having a so-called career."

Jenny kissed his cheek and said, "That's just one of the reasons why I love you so much. And you're a great dad, in spite of what you go through every day. But the kids do miss you, Jerry. If you got into another line of work, you could spend more time with them. Before they grow up and go away to college or something."

"I don't have a very clear idea of what else I'd like to do or what I'd be good at. I always wanted to be a homicide detective from the time I saw my first crime movie when I was about ten. It was pretty brutal, make my day and all that, but I saw past the Hollywood violence and realized that we really need people who work hard to solve crimes and bring some amount of closure."

"But there is no closure, is there?"

There was an ingrained practical side of her that wasn't susceptible to self-delusion, so he never tried to paper anything over. "No, honey," he admitted. "But there is often justice. And that's all that I can strive for."

Just then, Billy and Janie come running over and tossed their baseball gloves on a bench. "Dad, can we have some money for snow cones?" Janie pleaded. "I'm all sweaty and tired."

Billy yelled, "Me, too, Dad."

Smiling at how cute they looked in spite of the sweat-caked dirt on their smooth young faces, Jerry stood up, took out his wallet, and pulled out a twenty-dollar bill. "Get me a vanilla ice cream cone," he told them. "One for Mom, too."

The kids immediately took off, then Jenny called after them, "Hey! Make mine chocolate!"

She and Jerry both laughed, then he sat back down and put his arm around her.

"Would you ever want to go back into teaching?" Jenny asked, softly mentioning what she hoped for. She thought their lives had been more mellow back when Jerry was a high school English teacher and that maybe he shouldn't have gone into law enforcement.

"Well," he said, "I make more money as a cop, even though I may be in more danger—but maybe not, considering the epidemic of school shootings."

They fell silent, thinking about how they worried these days while the kids were in school. But they couldn't help smiling as they watched them paying for ice cream and snow cones and struggling to carry it all.

"These kinds of moments should last forever," Jerry said. "They're really what life is all about."

9

Vince Spivak and Melissa Kelter went to a different kind of park that day, a sprawling amusement park that was in Duquesne, Pennsylvania, across the river from Pittsburgh proper. It was called Kennywood and was one of the top amusement parks in the nation, which made it a source of local pride. She had grown up in Duquesne and had worked as a ticket-taker for one of the roller coaster rides. Vince had grown up in Clairton, not far from Duquesne, but his school picnics, from grade school on up, had always been at Kennywood, and so were all the other school picnics in Allegheny County.

"I haven't been here for a long time," Melissa said as they walked the fairway, she in blue shorts and a yellow blouse, and he in a T-shirt and blue jeans.

He wondered if he should hold her hand. But it seemed too teenybopper-like.

She said, "I don't know why I wanted to come here. I've been avoiding it like the plague."

"Why?"

"My brother picked on me anytime he saw me on one of the rides. He would try to jump into the seat next to me if he could, or else the one right behind me, then he'd pull my hair or put bubble gum in it or—worse— poke at me, grab me, unhook my seat belt if he could, and act like he was gonna throw me out. I used to try to hide from him in the Penny Arcade or I'd go through Noah's Ark over and over so he couldn't spot me."

"That rotten brat ruined your childhood!" Vince snarled. "It's a wonder he didn't turn you into a basket case. I hope we catch him and put him away."

"I hope you do, too," Melissa said. "I wasn't the only kid he picked on, but he was scared of the bigger boys, like the football players, so he never went near them. His victims of choice were smaller boys, usually much younger than him, or else girls."

"But somehow, he managed to land Jackie. Was she the timid clinging-violet type?"

"No, she was very self-assertive when he first started dating her and brought her home to meet my mom. He pulled the wool over her eyes. But he changed after they were married, and so did she. It was as if they traded places. She became a wimp, and he became dominant. She let him boss her around and beat on her. He made her feel like she deserved it."

"Typical victim pathology. Fear mixed with self-loathing."

"Oh god! That sounds so terrible!" Melissa said.

"Because it *is* terrible," Vince said. "It's what makes people stay in abusive relationships. The abuser makes them believe that they're so worthless that nobody but the abuser could ever love them. Some of them break the chains, and some never do."

"I don't want to stay here very long," said Melissa. "I just wanted to prove I could do it, like confronting the boogeyman."

"Well, let's at least get some cotton candy and try to be like the normal kids we never were," Vince said. "I mean kids who don't have any fear of bullies."

"You were scared of them too?"

"I would always fight back, so they learned to leave me alone. Also, I didn't like the encounters, so I tried to avoid them."

"I couldn't avoid Bradley because we lived together in the same house," Melissa said.

Vince knew she wouldn't want him to feel sorry for her, so he tried not to. She was young and beautiful, and he was glad to be with her.

There were throngs of folks of all ages everywhere they walked, past the "amusements"—which he didn't find as amusing or enthralling as they were when he was little. People were lining up for rides, climbing into turtle-shaped cars to have their bones rattled and their heads dizzied, or getting into roller coaster cars and then screaming and waving their hands in the air as if they were daring the plummeting cars to fly off the tracks while they were in them. Everywhere were the sounds of barkers, calliopes, little electrical cars with bumpers colliding, and targets being knocked over with guns or softballs. In the air was the heavy mouth-watering aroma of hot dogs, french fries, cotton candy, and much more. Most folks had smiles on their faces, but some of the parents looked dog-tired, and some of their kids were bawling or misbehaving.

After Vince and Melissa bought clouds of pink cotton candy on a stick and were walking along biting it and letting the sugary stuff melt on their tongues, Vince said, "George Romero, the Pittsburgh fellow who directed *Night of the Living Dead*, shot scenes from some of his other movies here, but I forget which ones."

"One of them was called *The Affair*," Melissa recalled. "I saw it on DVD a year or so ago, and I didn't think it was one of his best."

"I never saw it," Vince said. "But I bought a documentary on Romero, and one of the Blu-ray extras was a collection of some of his old TV spots, and one of them was a Kennywood spot featuring Kenny Kangaroo, one of their old mascots."

They both laughed, and Melissa said, "I'd like to see *that* one. There wasn't a Kenny Kangaroo when I worked here. I guess the character goes way back."

"All the way to the sixties," Vince informed her. "Do you want to get on one of the roller coasters just to prove that you can?"

"I might if we spot the Jack Rabbit. It's the one that used to terrify me the most when Bradley got on it behind me. But I haven't seen it. It must've been phased out."

"My favorite thing when I was a kid was riding the ponies. But it always was a letdown. They clomped along between narrowly spaced corral rails that prevented them from running loose—even if they could. I mean, most of them were probably way too old to gallop."

"Our childhoods sound kind of pathetic," Melissa said. "How did we ever become such accomplished adults after going through such angst?"

"I'm finding it boring," said Vince. "Let's get out of here and do something that's more fun."

"Like what?"

"I don't know. Just something," he said, glad that he didn't have to control the raging hormones of a teenager, just a rising desire to be with her more often and a hope that she might feel the same way.

10

On the following Monday, Spivak and Delaney were called out to a fresh crime scene. They arrived at it in an unmarked sedan, Spivak driving, and as they parked and got out of the car, the front door of the house swung open, and uniformed morgue attendants wheeled gurneys with body bags on them toward a coroner's van in the driveway.

Sheriff Donald Patton, in a brown suit instead of his uniform, came out and saw Spivak and Delaney. He was gray and balding, so he wore a neat goatee and mustache, perhaps to compensate. Approaching his two detectives, he said, "You guys got here fast, even though both of you live farther away than I do. I've been here with the two patrolmen for about an hour. You're too late to see them the way we found them, but you'll see the photos that CSI took. They're still dusting and going through the rest of their protocol, hoping to find fingerprints or DNA."

Spivak said, "Do you think whatever went down here might be related to what happened to Jackie Kelter?"

"Yeah, just due to the sheer brutality of the stabbing," the sheriff said. "Seems the killer couldn't stop himself. The husband, Ed Warner, was only shot once—a clean kill. But his wife, Mary, appears to have been butchered like Jackie Kelter must have been because of the large volume of blood evidence. We don't have crimes that violent around here, as a rule. That alone might tie the two cases together. If so, we have a serial killer operating in both right here in Allegheny County."

"A multiple-opportunity offender," Spivak quipped sourly.

"Just what we need," Delaney said just as sourly. "A wide section of a large county to work in and so far no clues to speak of."

"We'd better stick around in case the CSI team comes up with something, so we can jump on it right away," Spivak suggested.

Delaney said, "Yeah, but first, let's make a coffee run."

"I'll stay here till you get back," Sheriff Patton said. "Then I've got to head to the office for a meeting with the county commissioners. They're in a dither about this."

11

Sandy Jacobs was sitting in front of a surgeon, Dr. Francis Heller, who was facing her from behind the plain steel desk in his office, with a raft of professional certificates on the wall behind him. He was a middle-aged man with a pasty complexion, a shock of gray hair, and a thick gray mustache. He was wearing a black tie, a white lab coat, and large black-rimmed eyeglasses. Sandy was wearing tasteful makeup and jewelry, and she was in a form-fitting but conservative blue suit with a colorful scarf.

Dr. Heller eyed her closely and asked, "You haven't changed your mind, have you? You're definitely going ahead with the operation?"

She knew there was no reason to hold back anymore. The stolen coin collection had yielded $55,000 even after the exorbitant amount that went to the fence.

She said, "Of course, Dr. Heller. I've wanted this for a long time."

He nodded at her and said, "Well, you've been progressing nicely toward the desired result. I think you're more than ready in a physical and emotional sense and also in the lead-up to the transition."

Sandy smiled brightly for the doctor, knowing that her bright smile was a way of seeming less evil than she really was. It was a mask that she enjoyed putting on for everyone. "I'm more than ready," she affirmed. "Tell me what I need to know."

Dr. Heller lit up a big flat screen on the wall to the left of his desk, and Sandy focused her attention on graphic medical illustrations of the nitty-gritty behind sex change operations as her surgeon expounded on them in a dry, pedantic monotone.

"Now, what is commonly called a sex change involves reshaping the male genitals into the appearance of and, as far as possible, the functions of female genitalia. The testicles are of course surgically removed, and the skin and foreskin of the penis is inverted, preserving blood vessels and nerve endings to form a fully sensitive vagina. A clitoris is formed from part of the glans of the penis. Other scrotal tissue is used to form the labia majora."

On the flat screen appeared all that the doctor was explaining, including a full-color close-up of the surgically formed vagina.

Sandy is reassured by how authentic it looks. She said, "It looks perfect! Will I get a similar result? What are you willing to say about that?"

"Well...I must caution you," said Dr. Heller. "That since this surgery requires existing skin formations, it's never an exact procedure. The aesthetic, functional, and sensitivity aspects of vaginoplasty vary greatly—and can be complicated by problems such as blood loss, infections, or nerve damage."

"Gosh! What else?" Sandy asked, somewhat alarmed.

Dr. Heller said, "Lubrication is needed during sex, and occasional douching is advised so bacteria do not grow and give off odors. Furthermore, because of the risk of vaginal stenosis, which is a narrowing or loss of flexibility of the vagina, a patient may need to use a vaginal expander to keep the vagina open."

"What about doing that in…other ways?"

"I assume you mean penile penetration with a sex partner, but regretfully that is not an adequate method of performing dilation."

Sandy softly said with some amusement, "I'm sorry to hear that, Doctor."

He said, "I'm glad you're maintaining your sense of humor. A bad attitude isn't helpful going into any sort of surgical procedure."

"I have a question," she said. "If I keep taking estrogen, can anything be done about my small breasts?"

"Oftentimes, the hormonal therapy would have done better for you. But, if you wish, we can schedule a breast augmentation, no different from a procedure for any other woman, and you should increase by one to two cup sizes."

"You told me that once before, but I wanted to revisit the subject. How soon can we schedule my primary surgery?"

"I'd say within two weeks. I'll be in touch so we can confirm it."

"Very good," said Sandy, glad that she would be getting what she had long wanted.

12

After her session with Dr. Heller, Sandy, and Bradley were in a booth in a saloon, drinking beer and munching fresh, thick potato chips that were deep-fried on the premises.

She started telling him about her gender-conflicted childhood.

"I pretty much knew that I was different, but I didn't know if I could tell anyone how I felt without being ridiculed or shunned. Then when I was twelve, I read an article in *People* magazine about a teenage boy saying he felt like he was trapped in the wrong body, and that's when I started to admit to myself that I was the same way."

"So what did you do about it?" Bradley asked with an uncaring bluntness that always annoyed her.

"Nothing. I did nothing about it," she said. "Except punish myself, and hate myself. And bust a gut trying to keep up with other boys my age and act as masculine as they were. But at the same time, I was secretly wearing some of my mother's clothes when she and my dad weren't at home. We lived in Youngstown, Ohio, and he was a rough and tough mill worker. If he ever got the slightest idea I might be gay, he would've beat me up and kicked me out of the house. So I went out for the high school track team and did other stuff like that. Then I enlisted in the Marine Corps, and he was proud of me. But I never went home again after I was discharged."

"Why?"

"I got a taste for killing while I was in Afghanistan. And at the same time, I started to wonder why I had to keep acting like a man. I learned about the transsexual thing, and I felt like that's what I wanted to do. But at first I just began dressing female and going out more often in that gender."

"So you started as a transvestite?"

"Not all the time at first, just on occasion, when the impulse overcame me."

They both fell silent for a moment.

Then Sandy eyes Bradley and hits him with a question of her own. "So what was *your* childhood like? Did you always have a mean streak? Or didn't you realize you had it in you?"

"When I was in grade school, I was a wimp around other people, but I picked on my sister because she was there, and she was easy. As time went by, I branched out, especially after I built myself up by lifting weights and made the football team. I started to keep my eye open for the kinds of boys who seemed vulnerable, the kind who badly wanted to be my pal because I was a jock with a football letter and sweater. I got better and better at preying on their weaknesses. I could usually suck them in if I put my mind to it, even if they started out seeming to be strong and independent. Jackie was a prime example of that. Almost anybody's self-image can be eroded if you're clever and persistent enough. But first, you have to make them trust you."

"You sound as devious as I am," Sandy said. "How did you get that way?"

Bradley took a big gulp of beer and stayed locked in his thoughts for a long time while Sandy waited to see if he was going to open up to her. She had extraordinary patience because she was a skilled manipulator, more so than he was.

Finally, with a faraway look in his eyes, he started to divulge things. He said, "I'm going to tell you something I've never told anyone else. When I was in the Cub Scouts, I was molested by someone who was close to my father, his best friend, in fact. He was also the Cub Scout leader. My parents trusted him so much that they let him take me to the movies and on camping trips and such, usually with the rest of the troop, but sometimes not. I looked up to him. He was so charismatic he could've been a preacher—I mean a Jim Jones type, the type that can make his followers drink Kool-Aid laced with cyanide. But I couldn't stand him touching me, much less putting his thing in my mouth...or other places where it hurt. But I was scared to tell anybody. I thought my father wouldn't believe me over his best friend. I thought if I had been born a girl, like my sister, he wouldn't be doing those things to me. That's when I started taking it out on her."

"Was your abuser simultaneously your role model in some ways?" Sandy wanted to know.

"I guess he was. He liked having kids look up to him, probably because most adults didn't. He was a lowly guy at his job, a school custodian, a janitor, a nobody. But with us little boys, he was like a guardian, a drill master, and a chaplain all rolled into one. I don't think the Cub Scouts are supposed to be about religion, but he'd preach to us. He died when I was only fourteen, but by that time, he had made me secretly hate myself."

"Did you go to college?"

"No, I managed to graduate from high school with grades that weren't totally terrible, and I was jealous of my sister, Melissa, because she was always on the Honor Roll and had so many friends. Like I said, I played football but not well enough to get a scholarship, even to a small college. Mostly I played because I liked ramming into people and knocking them down as hard as I could. I liked to try to break bones, and I succeeded a couple of times. But for me, college was out of the question. After graduation, I went to work on an assembly line in a bottling plant, and that's where I was still working when I was with Jackie. She kept pushing me to better myself by going to night school, but I didn't want to."

Sandy said, "You and I have a lot in common. We both had messed up childhoods. In my case, I think it was worse. At least you had no problem growing up male —right?"

"Like I told you, I picked on my sister because she didn't have some old man victimizing her sexually, like I did. Because of what was done to me, I hated gays. So I went out with other straight guys and beat up the homosexuals who cruised the streets in the rough sections of downtown. If we would've run across you in those days, we'd have probably mugged you and rolled you and left you in a gutter."

Sandy said, with a flash of anger, "That's what *you* think, tough guy! There was a woman inside of me, but on the outside, I was hard and mean. That's how I survived in combat. Not all my kills were justified either."

"And you're still killing people when it suits you," Bradley said admiringly. "Do you think you'll quit once your gender is to your liking?"

"I don't know. Maybe I'll like it even more."

"I understand that. I like it, too. I can't wait for your friend to get here so we can get started on another money kill."

Sandy looked toward the entrance of the saloon, perked up, and said, "Speak of the devil. She's right on time. Here she comes now."

An attractive, well-dressed woman in her thirties swept the place, fastened her eyes on them, and came directly to their booth.

Sandy said, "Have a seat, Norma. Bradley, this is the woman I told you about, Norma Harris."

Norma sat and briefly took Bradley's hand in hers. She said, "I need a drink. I've never done anything like this before."

Sandy smiled and said, "I'll get you one. Gin and tonic, the usual?"

"Yeah, thanks. Does it get added to your fee?" Norma quipped.

"Fringe benefit," Sandy said, and they both chuckled as Sandy pivoted and headed to the bar.

Norma eyed Bradley piercingly, saying, "So...you're the one who's going to do the job for me?"

"Me and Sandy. Yeah."

"I suppose I can trust you if she does."

Sandy came back with a gin and tonic and placed it before Norma. Having overheard Norma's comment, she said, "You can trust us both, Norma. We're professionals."

Norma said, "I'm glad you opened up to me about your extracurricular activities and offered to solve my problem for me. I can give you the five grand up front. The rest you'll get when I collect my husband's insurance."

"The full fifty thousand?" Sandy said to make sure.

"Everything we agreed on, Sandy. I'm not a grifter," Norma assured her. "But I want it to look like an accident, so my kids will have an easier time getting over it. I don't want a bloody murder, nothing that will give them nightmares. They're young and never had to face real grief."

This comment hit home for Bradley Kelter because he had been so lost in his own feelings about Jackie that he had pushed certain things out of his mind. He had concentrated on making sure that he got his mother's promise that she would take care of his children and that she would never let Melissa get custody of them, no matter how hard Melissa might try. He inwardly congratulated himself that he had taken these noble steps to make sure of his children's future and thus had assuaged his guilt over what he was going to do to their mother. Since he had had much experience in fighting off guilt, he felt that any remnants of it would ease up over time.

He came out of his reverie as Sandy said to Norma, "We can make it look like a hit and run. How's that?"

"That'd be perfect," Norma said with a smile. "I thought of staging a car wreck because he drives too fast all the time, even when he's not intoxicated. In a way, I'm doing this for the children. My girls are five and seven. They'll have a better chance of not dying in a car accident if they don't have to ever be in a car with their drunken father."

"That's a good way of looking at it. I can respect that," Bradley interjected.

Norma flashed him an odd look, then said, "Okay. So how soon can it happen?"

Sandy said, "You clue us in to where he's going to be and when, and we'll do the job. It can be done when you need it to be."

Norma didn't take long replying, which made it obvious that she had already thought this out. She said, "Two days from now, he has a dinner engagement with a client at a good Italian restaurant, his favorite. And it's on a dark, narrow street. And the parking garage he uses isn't far from it, and after the dinner, he'll be drunk when he goes for his car."

"Perfect," said Sandy. "We'll do it outside the parking garage. We'll use your Jeep, Bradley. But we'll put a stolen plate on it."

They finished their drinks, making plans to meet together one last time before pulling off the hit-and-run, so Norma could pay the advance, and they could make sure there wouldn't be any glitches.

When she was gone, Bradley remained lost in thought for a while, then he said, "This is exciting stuff. I like it because we're doing something important for the customer. But it made me start thinking about some-thing else I'd like to do."

"What would that be?" Sandy asked expectantly.

"My sister, Melissa. She's unfinished business. I'm sure you can understand that, Sandy. She's unfinished business that I'd like to deal with once and for all. If my mom dies, she might end up with my children, and she might treat them badly as a way of getting even with me."

"My, my, Bradley, you don't have much faith in

people, do you?" Sandy said with a wry grin. "Let's see how it goes with Norma's husband. Then maybe we can turn our attention to your sister. I suppose you'll expect me to act as your accomplice pro bono."

"That'd be nice," said Bradley. "And fun for us both. Right?"

13

S andy Jacobs got dressed in style to go to Jackie Kelter's funeral. She wore a dark blue dress, sheer nylons, delicate golden earrings, and a gold necklace consisting of a little gold cross on an exquisitely fine, thin chain. She had taken a bath in lilac-scented water, and after she had thoroughly dried herself with a thick, plush towel half as big as her silk bedspread and blow-dried, brushed and combed her light-brown shoulder-length hair, parting it on the left side and letting it fall to her shoulders, she had dabbed the backs of her ears with Estee Lauder.

She wanted to attract admiration but not stares.

Foolishly, Bradley had wanted to come to the church with her, but she had told him off. Did he want to be spotted, chased down and beat up or killed? Or turned over to the police? He was turning into too much of a chance-taker. Having gotten away with a whole lot up to this point, he was starting to think of himself as some sort of modern swashbuckler. Or like a Ted Bundy who could go for years without getting unmasked.

In other words, he was a loose cannon. Which made Sandy think that their partnership might not be destined to last very long.

She deliberately waited for five or six minutes till the church totally filled up before she made an unobtrusive entrance and sat in the back, in the last pew at the end closest to the aisle. She and Bradley had read Jackie's obituary online, so she was aware that the coffin had been closed during a one-day viewing at the funeral home, and of course it was closed now and would be closed when the hearse drove it to the cemetery to be interred. Right now, the mourners were enduring the rigmarole of a Catholic Mass, and the coffin was draped with a tapestry.

Sandy discreetly looked the crowd over while the priest droned on. She spotted two guys sitting together in the pew across the aisle, and she pegged them as plainclothes cops. This made her chuckle inwardly because she knew that law officers often attended funerals in the hope that the murderer of the deceased would also dare to and do something inadvertently that would cause himself to be spotted. Or in Sandy's case, *her*self, not himself. She had nothing to do with Jackie's death, of course, but she knew from a TV report that detectives named Delaney and Spivak were not only investigating Jackie's case but also the robbery and murder of Ed and Mary Warner. She peered more closely at her side view of the two purported cops in the pew across the aisle and ascertained to her satisfaction that, yes, they were, in fact, Spivak and Delaney.

When at last the Mass was over, and the priest finished shaking sweet, pungent incense around in a fancy silver incense urn, the mourners began to make their exit down the center of the church, with the coffin and pallbearers in the lead, followed first by family members of the deceased, then the rest of them. The cop named Spivak exited his pew and took the elbow of Bradley's sister, Melissa, whom Sandy recognized from a wallet photo that Bradley had shown her. It was a picture of her at age sixteen or so, and now she looked even classier and prettier. She had the classy bearing that Sandy aspired to. The cop named Delaney exited the church a little behind Melissa and Spivak—and it dawned on Sandy that somehow the cop and the murderer's sister had now become an item. She watched as the rest of the mourners trudged down the center aisle en masse, folding in on themselves from the altar on down, making Sandy and the couple of others in her pew the last to trickle out.

It was a bright summer day, and Sandy stood by herself on the steps of the church, knowing that she cut a fine figure in her stylish apparel and not minding if she drew attention from some of the gentlemen in attendance. No one here had reason to suspect her of a crime.

That other detective, the one whose last name was Delaney, was nowhere in sight, and Sandy figured he must have been anxious to head home. She had researched him and knew that he was a family man with a wife and two children. Handy to know in case he ever got too hot on her trail, and she should need a way to threaten him.

She watched the pallbearers putting the casket into the hearse as the mourners headed for their cars and SUVs. Each vehicle lined up in front of the church bore a funeral flag. The priest was helping Jackie's mother into a seat in the hearse when she stared at Melissa Kelter and that detective named Spivak and yelled, "Why the hell are you here, you smug bitch! To gloat over your evil brother's handiwork? You've got your nerve! I better not see you at the wake or I'll pull your hair out!"

Spivak grabbed Melissa's arm tighter and turned her from Jackie's angry, grieving mom and hustled her away from there.

Sandy had no intention of being at the wake and didn't even know where it would take place. No doubt it would be announced after the prayers in the cemetery. But she wasn't going to the cemetery either. She had seen enough to be able to report to Bradley that his sister not only had the nerve to be at the church but also must be having a fling with one of the detectives. It was fast work on her part. His, too.

Bradley had expressed what normal people would call "a sick urge" to kill Melissa, and when he found out she was screwing a cop, the urge would probably become insurmountable. Sandy well understood how those types of urges worked and were enhanced. She was glad she would be helping Bradley satisfy that whim. She could prevent him from doing it in a rash way and getting them both caught.

She thought it would be nice to torture and kill Melissa's detective friend too. It might even slow up the investigation. And it would please Bradley no end. She wanted to keep him happy for as long as she needed him. Happy and compliant, which was the way she liked all of her men.

She came down from the church steps, intentionally not making contact with any of the mourners, whose numbers were quickly dwindling as they departed for the cemetery. She walked around the corner to a parking spot a block away, where her truck was. It was old and dirty and did not have a funeral flag on it, and it would not have gone well with her attire or her demeanor.

She decided not to head back to her farm right away for fear of getting held up by the parade of mourners with their police escorts holding up all the other traffic. It was a perfect interlude for her to dine at one of her favorite bistros and show herself off to the ritzy clientele. She thought that maybe an elegant, wealthy gentleman might hit on her. Such was her ultimate aim, once her upcoming operation made her into the complete woman that she knew she was always meant to be, to land a husband who was cultured and rich.

First there had to be a Number One. And after that, there could be a string of them, each one making her wealthier and wealthier.

She wanted to become an elegant, mysterious world traveler. She figured she could meet a lot of eligible guys on cruise ships.

It was the kind of life she deserved.

14

The day of Jackie Kelter's funeral was a Saturday, and Jerry Delaney was taking the rest of the day off to go with Jenny and Janie to Billy's Little League game, then to McDonald's, and then his plan was to hole up in his home office to review the Murder Books on Jackie Kelter's presumed murder and the murders of Ed and Mary Warner. But first, right after the funeral, he had to spend some time with his mother, who was in a nursing home, suffering from dementia that wasn't officially labeled as Alzheimer's. He had learned that the only way that Alzheimer's could be definitively diagnosed was through autopsy. But in his mother's case, all the recognizable symptoms were present and had become gradually more undeniable until he had to take steps to get her into Kane Hospital, a nursing facility in McKeesport, six miles from White Oak, where Jerry lived with his family and was trying to make their lives much more normal and peaceful than his had been.

His father had been a Jekyll-and-Hyde alcoholic who terrorized him and his mother all through his growing-up years, and the worry and the terror had continued even when through college and into his time in the army. But his mother had stuck it out with his father, much as Jackie Kelter apparently had done. His own experiences with that sort of manipulation and spousal abuse were an ingrained part of his drive to find Jackie's husband and bring him to justice for the murder he had apparently committed.

All through the early years of his marriage, especially after his first child was born, Jerry and his wife Jenny had done all they could to get her out of her house and briefly bestow a few moments of happiness away from her husband, who was continuing to make her life miserable. When he thought deeply about the situation, Jerry had vague hopes that if one of his elderly parents had to pass away ahead of the other one, the first one to go might be his father, so his mother would enjoy just a few of the years in a person's life that was supposed to be "golden."

He felt guilty even having such thoughts, but they were realized when his father died basically of alcoholism at age 67.

Jerry never would have wished death on anyone, especially his father or mother. All his life, he had yearned for a more wholesome relationship with his dad as father and son, but Gerald Delaney, Sr.'s death had cruelly ended those hopes. A few weeks after his father's passing, Jerry had a dream in which he had encountered his father on the street where he had grown up and had hugged him and said pleadingly, "I love you, Dad, and I want us to be friends." And in his dream, his dad had replied, "I don't know what you mean." When he awoke, he looked at a photo of his father as a bright, handsome young man fifteen years before Jerry was even born, and through Jerry's mind swept a cascade of anguished thoughts of how different things would have been if alcohol had never gotten its hold on him.

He and Jenny would take his mom with them on short vacations and on one-day excursions to amusement parks, picnic areas, and historical sites, with which the Pittsburgh area abounded. Places like the Henry Clay Frick Mansion, the Fort Pitt Museum, and Fort Necessity, where young Colonel George Washington had been forced to surrender his sword to the French during the outbreak of the French and Indian War. Jerry's mother greatly enjoyed every second she was able to spend with Jerry and Jenny and later with both of their children.

But one day they noticed that his mom, in her early seventies, began not taking care of herself very hygienically. She stopped taking regular baths and started to smell bad. Jerry began to phone her an hour or so prior to picking her up at her house to go on various excursions, so he could prompt her, as delicately as he could, to have herself bathed and ready when he got there.

She would say each time, "Yes, I already took my shower," but it became all too apparent that she actually hadn't.

Then one day, after dropping his mom off for a checkup at her doctor's office, Jerry and Jenny decided to clean her house for her, because it too was starting to smell and was terribly unkempt in a way that had never happened before. And when they piled dishes in the sink to be washed and dried, then bent to get dishwashing soap out of the kitchen cabinet, they saw a chicken that his mom must have put in there, uncooked and smelling horrible. Obviously, in her mind, she had put the chicken into the refrigerator.

This was the shocking revelation that brought home

to Jerry that something was wrong with his mom, mentally. And from there, it was all downhill, gradually at first, but then gaining momentum. In those beginning stages of her disease, she was lucid enough to give Jerry her power of attorney, which he used to get her into a personal care home, which was not a full-fledged nursing home but a room in a private home where she was given room, board and medical attention in return for her monthly social security check. Well and good as a stop-gap, but it didn't suffice for long. Within a year or so, it became clear that she needed to go to a more state-of-the-art full-service facility, and Jerry did all the necessary paperwork to get her a higher level of care at Kane Hospital, covered by the Commonwealth of Pennsylvania, which was fortunate because there was no way either she or her son could have paid the staggering costs, which amounted to thousands of dollars per month.

By now, Jerry's mom had been a patient there for two years and had slowly worsened to the point where she no longer recognized him. The closest she ever came to any sort of recognition was when she thought he was her brother, who had died in the Vietnam War. Jerry didn't bother trying to correct her when she called him by his late uncle's name, which was Richard. Meaningful conversation didn't happen between them anymore; she scarcely knew he was there. The best he could do was to visit her every other week, stay for about a half hour in monotonously uncomfortable silence, look for a chance to talk with a doctor or some of the nurses to assure himself that she was being well taken care of, then kiss her on her cheek and slink out of her ward, remembering to make sure that the code-operated door was tightly closed, otherwise some of the dementia sufferers would walk out, sometimes managing to make it all the way into the surrounding neighborhood in their robes and pajamas—or even without them. usually heading home or to the police station or to a bar for a few drinks, feeling vaguely guilty. Six months ago, she became unable to feed herself, and Jerry had to sign a form allowing a surgical team to perform a procedure whereby a hole was made in her stomach, and a feeding tube was inserted. It broke his heart every time he saw her this way.

On this particular Saturday, after Jackie Kelter's graveside ceremony was over, he drove to the huge monolithic yellow-brick suburban hospital and took an elevator up to the sixth floor, where the Alzheimer's patients were housed—or, as some would say, *ware*housed. He had to search his memory for the four-digit code that made the wide double doors swing open, admitting him to his mom's wing. He anticipated that he would be there for a stultifying, utterly depressing short visit, as usual. But when he sat and peered over the safety rails on his mom's bed, she appeared to be going in and out of a deep, hazy slumber, then for the first time he saw that there were bloody sores on her legs, which shocked him into action. He rushed out to find a nurse, and when he encountered one in the hall, he blurted angrily, "What in the world is going on with my mother? Don't you people know she has bed sores? Don't you keep her bathed and in clean bedding like you're supposed to? You're supposed to make sure she turns over now, and then so her skin doesn't get rubbed raw!"

The nurse looked startled and apologetic, and he thought she was reacting with shame for her lack of attentiveness. But then she explained. "What you've seen, Jerry, aren't bed sores. Oftentimes, patients become allergic to the liquid food we have to feed them through the tube. When that happens, we have nothing else to resort to. Their body becomes hypersensitive to the nutrients and sores start breaking out all over their bodies. You're going to have an awful decision to make."

He was dumbstruck by this news. And the nurse went on to say that he might have to give permission for the staff to stop making his mother ingest food through a tube.

"What procedure can we adapt to?" he asked despairingly.

And he got the answer he dreaded.

"I'm afraid there is nothing else we can offer right now," the nurse said. "Her organs are rejecting her nutrients. Please don't let a lot of time go by. Phone for an appointment with Dr. Morgan within the next few days. He'll inform you of your options."

But Jerry already knew, from what she had already said, that there would be no good options, no technological salvation. If he had to give instructions for his mom not to be fed through that tube anymore, it would be the same as taking her off of life support.

For the time being, he had to pull himself together and steel himself not to betray his sadness and regret over a situation that he could not change. Every day on the job he had to deal with the ugly side of life, and he tried hard to shield his wife and children from the danger and the unfairness. He wanted Billy and Janie to embrace all the good things that life could offer. He wanted them to grow up happy and hopeful and well-grounded enough to face the worst that might come later. Jerry knew well that there were no guarantees in life except the unconditional love and guidance that he and Jenny could guarantee as parents.

15

B radley Kelter had an inkling that Sandy Jacobs was more intelligent than he was. But at least he was smart enough to know, just as well as she did, that there was no honor among thieves. He firmly believed in the evil-doers' Golden Rule: Do unto others before they do unto you.

He was itching to kill Sandy Jacobs and grab all the money she had gotten from the murder of the coin guy and the hit on Peter Harris, but for now, he was biding his time and waiting for the perfect opportunity. Sandy had given Bradley a mere five thousand as his share of the loot from fencing the coin collection, and she had said that she was going to give him a bigger slice— $20,000—from the insurance payout that would be collected by Peter's wife, Norma. But that was peanuts compared to the haul Sandy intended to keep for herself. Bradley was not only disappointed, he was angry, but sneaky enough not to show it. He figured that the two jobs combined would put as much as two hundred thousand into Sandy's stash. And he wanted to figure out a way to take all of it. A pal of his back when they used to beat up gay men that they'd let blow them before taking their wallets and jewelry was fond of saying, "I might have my mom's features, but I have my daddy's fixtures, and I'm not confused about it." Then he'd let loose with a laugh that was loud and coarse like the braying of a mule.

Well, Bradley realized that Sandy wasn't confused about her gender either. She knew what she wanted and what she didn't want. She knew she wanted to be a girl. It had just taken her a long time to get there. Now she was going to finish the transformation. She wanted tits but not balls. Her Adam's apple had already been shaved down. Soon her testicles would go bye-bye, maybe into a hazardous waste bin, and her dick would be turned inside out to serve as a makeshift vagina. The thought of it made Bradley ill. It made his balls shrivel up into his groin, just as they did whenever he thought of getting kicked in them.

———

ON THE EVENING of their hit on Peter Harris, Sandy and Bradley were lying in wait for him, parked near his parking garage in Bradley's Jeep. They were smoking a joint and passing it back and forth and Bradley said, "You probably noticed that I like living a life of crime, Sandy. It's exciting all the time, never boring, and the pay is good—better than being a warehouse flunky like I was before. I feel like I understand career criminals in a way I didn't used to. The loud-mouthed politicians should try it before they go blathering on and on about it."

She laughed at his self-proclaimed "wisdom" and crude insights.

"Well," she said, "you started your career on your own when you turned on your wife. But I've been helping you enter a new phase where you don't do it for free, you actually make money off of it."

He exhaled a lung full of smoke while he let this sink in. Then he said, "Yeah, I guess you could say I'm matchiculating. And it's a blast."

"Ma*tric*ulating," she said, correcting his mispronunciation. "You should become—"

She was going to say "more cultured," but she had to clam up. "Here he comes!" she blurted. "That's him! Start the engine!"

They gaped at a dapper-looking businessman who was wobbling a bit as he appeared a block away on the semi-dark street.

Bradley turned the key in the ignition, and the Jeep moved forward.

Peter Harris stopped walking as soon as he was hit with the bright headlights.

Sandy yelled, "*Gun it*, Bradley!"

He put the pedal to the metal and swerved the Jeep up over the curb and onto the sidewalk.

SMASH! Peter Harris was helplessly frozen in the glare of the headlights and got crushed and run over at a devastatingly high speed.

The Jeep careened and bounced back over the curb, then sped away into the night.

Bradley and Sandy laughed uproariously.

As Bradley drove furiously, hunched over the wheel with clenched fingers, Sandy said

"Boom!" and made a hand motion imitating a body being knocked and hurtled through space.

16

After he met with Dr. Morgan, who was his mother's primary physician, and a staff of five other doctors and nurses, Jerry Delaney headed to a local bar where Vince Spivak and Melissa Kelter were waiting for him. Two days ago, Jerry had confided to Vince about the grim purpose of the meeting, and Vince and Melissa were heartsick about it and wanted to give as much comfort and support as they could.

The Terrace Lounge in McKeesport, not far from Kane Hospital, was a hang out for cops, but right now, at eleven in the morning on a Tuesday, it wasn't very lively, and Jerry was relieved because he didn't want to muster up any false camaraderie with colleagues. He spotted Vince and Melissa in a booth, walked over to them as if he had the weight of the world on his shoulders, murmured a sad hello, and sat down across from them as Vince poured him a draft beer from a pitcher that was going flat.

"I'm not going to ask how it went," Vince said. "I can tell by the look on your face."

"It hit me hard even though I expected it," Jerry said. "I guess a part of me was still trying to hold out hope."

"Oh, I'm so sorry," Melissa murmured and reached out to lay her hand on top of Jerry's.

"I had to give them permission to stop feeding her," Jerry said, struggling to hold back tears. "Dr. Morgan left it to me to make the decision, but really I no longer had a choice." He wiped his eyes and swallowed some of his beer. "Her body is rejecting her food and trying to force-feed her would only make her break out in more sores, and they're going to bleed and likely become infected. But they told me that withholding food won't cause her to die quickly or painlessly. They said that the nutrition she was getting through the feeding tube was optimal, therefore, withholding it would cause her to deteriorate very slowly. In effect, she would starve to death, and the process wouldn't be quick. It would probably take five or six weeks."

"Oh my god! That's terrible!" Melissa exclaimed.

Vince said, "I'm here for you, buddy."

Jerry knew there wasn't much they could do to help him get through it. He had to somehow find the words to tell his wife and kids, and he had no idea how or if they would be able to cope. "Life is what happens when you're making other plans," he said. "Like other trite sayings, it's trite because it's so true that people keep repeating it."

"You can't help being flippant even when you've been hit hard," Vince said.

"Yeah, I'm a real jokester," Jerry said miserably.

"Would a leave of absence do you any good?" Vince ventured to ask. "I'd be willing to handle our caseload."

Jerry said, "Too much time to dwell on the situation would probably make me eat my gun." Then he saw the look of alarm on Melissa's face and said, "Don't worry, I don't mean it. I realize that my wife and kids need me, and I know that when a person kills himself, it gives his loved ones permission to do the same. That's why it runs in families. Ernest Hemingway and his father, brother, and one of his sisters committed suicide. Yet when I was an English major, I read quite a few of his novels and bought into the macho image he had created for himself."

"Me, too," said Melissa. "As a college freshman, I read some of his short stories, and I was impressed. They were very masculine but also sweet and poignant. But I never knew much about him beyond that."

Jerry said, "I was stunned when I learned he had died by putting a shotgun in his mouth and pulling both triggers. He was only sixty-two, but his health was failing. And so was his self-image, apparently. He probably bought into his own self-promotion, and when he felt that he could no longer live up to it, he took himself out."

"I watched that old movie on TCM," Vince said. "*The Sun Also Rises.*"

"I did too," said Jerry. "And I also read the novel. Hemingway believed that an author should always know something about his central character that he doesn't divulge to the reader. He said that every good novel is a mystery and not revealing everything enhances the intrigue."

"That's too deep for me," Vince said.

"Oh, honey, don't pretend you're dumb when Jerry and I know otherwise," Melissa said.

Jerry said, "It was barely hinted at in the movie, but while reading the novel, you become aware that Jake is impotent because when he was an infantryman in the First World War, he lost his testicles to a grenade or a land mine."

"Yikes!" Vince Spivak said. "Let's stop talking about it."

17

I ronically, Vince Spivak and Melissa Kelter had been followed to the Terrace Lounge by Bradley Kelter and Sandy Jacobs. The irony was that Sandy was looking forward to giving *up* her male parts while Jerry, Vince, and Melissa were discussing a literary figure created by Ernest Hemingway who had suffered that same fate *un*willingly.

Sandy had agreed to help Bradley capture, torture, and kill his sister, but now that Melissa was with two cops, not just one, Sandy decided that discretion trumped valor, so she insisted that they should wait for a more opportune time.

"I don't like blowin' this chance," Bradley argued. "I say we follow them when they leave. The cops might drop her off at her apartment, and then we're home free."

He was itching to put his sister through the agony he felt she deserved. Under his truck seat he had a kit containing zip ties, gloves, duct tape, pliers, a serrated hunting knife, and a soldering iron. He wanted to use these implements to patiently and sadistically ravage and destroy everything about Melissa that was female. He might even rape her because after she was dead, the hazards of incestuous birth would be null and void.

He envisioned that two days from now, after Sandy got the payoff from the Peter Harris job, he could kill the he or she or whatever she was, then take all her money and head for Alaska or maybe Mexico. Lately she was being so bitchy and contrary that he wanted to put his hands around her throat.

"Go after Melissa on your own if you've got ants in your pants," she told him. "But I'm not taking that chance. I'm going home, and I'm taking the truck. I don't mind helping you, but I'm not a fool. Make your mind up because I'm getting out of here."

"Damn it, all right already," Bradley said, scowling at her, but deciding that he didn't dare to attack his sister without Sandy operating not only as a lookout but as a willing participant.

"C'mon," she said. "Let's go get chops and fries."

Grouchily, he pulled out, made a U-turn, and headed for the barbecue joint. He drove without a word, thinking about reversing his plan. Maybe he should kill Sandy first, *then* his sister. In the disappointment of the moment, that seemed to make perfect sense.

18

Driving home, dreading that he had to break the news about his mom to his wife and kids, Jerry hoped they would handle their dire situation much better than the Hemingways had handled theirs. The suicides of Ernest's father and uncle, in particular, had produced a legacy of mental torture, suffering, and self-loathing that persisted over the course of several generations, wreaking bizarre, unpredictable trauma and tragedy.

On the night before he died, Ernest Hemingway's youngest son, Gregory, wore a demure black cocktail dress to a small private party in Coconut Grove, Florida. He introduced himself to some of his close friends as "Vanessa," and they took his latest episode of cross-dressing as a harmless lark or, at worst, a manifestation, at age sixty-nine, of mental anguish due to the loss of his medical license and a chain of divorces from his four ex-wives.

On the day after his "coming out" as Vanessa, he was spotted in Key Biscayne, walking down a main avenue, naked, and with a dress and high heels in his hand. A law officer took him into custody after filling out a report stating that the "publicly naked person of indeterminate gender" seemed to be "mentally unstable," and charging him with indecent exposure and resisting arrest. A medical exam while he was in jail revealed that he had undergone a sex change. He was therefore transferred to the cell block reserved for women.

Six days later, getting dressed for a court appearance, he collapsed onto the concrete floor and died.

One of his obituaries noted that his death, while tragic, had avoided the dire Hemingway family legacy of suicide. His friends said that he suffered from manic depression and a chemical imbalance that must have been hereditary since his father, his paternal grandfather and his uncle, aunt and niece had all committed suicide.

One of his psychiatrists revealed that Gregory's life-long flirtation with femininity had enraged his famous father and led to constant father-son confrontations that scarred Gregory as a boy and haunted him as an adult. At Ernest's insistence, he had undergone hundreds of shock treatments which never quite "cured" him of his chaotic childhood, a complex relationship with his mother, and an overwhelming desire for acceptance by his "macho" father.

"My father badly wanted a daughter," Gregory wrote in his memoir of Ernest in 1979, "so when I was born male, my mother felt that she had blown her last chance to make her lovable egomaniac happy. And she blamed me as much as she blamed herself as if I had chosen to be born that way. By the same token, my father blamed me for my mother's death because she collapsed and died after violently arguing with me over my gender."

On the day that Ernest Hemingway was buried,

Gregory/Vanessa said, "In a way, it's a great relief that he won't be around for me to disappoint him."

As bizarre as the trajectory of the Hemingway family was, Jerry Delaney could see some lessons in it for more ordinary kinds of families. How different would it have been if Ernest and Pauline, his fourth wife, had lovingly accepted Gregory and had refrained from heaping guilt and disparagement upon him for not being the daughter that they thought they had wanted?

With respect to his own son and daughter, Jerry always tried to live by his understanding that there were only two things that a parent could give to a child: Dreams and wounds.

He was keenly aware that he was on his way to deliver wounds, and he hoped that his son and daughter would not kill the messenger.

19

B radley and Sandy were exuberant, waiting for Norma Harris to show up with the payoff for the murder of her husband. They toasted one another, clinking shot glasses of whisky and tossing the whisky down with beer chasers as they rehashed their moment of glory.

"I saw his face in the headlights for a split second just before we plowed into him,"

Bradley proudly boasted. "I swear, he looked like he knew he was doomed "

Sandy said, "We did him a favor. It's not a bad way to go. Better than dying of old age, all feeble and decrepit. Like from cirrhosis, which Norma said he was heading for, or something even more awful, like cancer."

Bradley couldn't contain his glee as he poured himself another shot and downed it with a look of pain on his face as it hit his tonsils, which he squelched with another chug of beer. "It was great!" he enthused. "The look on his face! I always like to go to sleep reliving it, Sandy! I think we're made for each other. Don't you?" He didn't really mean that; he only said it to make her believe he valued her so much that he would never turn on her.

Sandy bought into it, seemingly. She told him, "We're a good team, and we're going to split our first big score. Norma is bringing a cashier's check for fifty thousand. I'm going to give you twenty of it. Now I can afford my operation. But it doesn't happen till two weeks from now, and it's going to take a long time to heal. After that, we can be friends with benefits. But in the meantime, you'll need someone young and pretty, so we'll have to go hunting. You'll like *that*, won't you, Bradley?"

She laughed tipsily and mischievously.

Bradley said, "You're not fooling me. If we capture a pretty young female, you're gonna want her as badly as I do."

And so, two days later, Sandy and Bradley rented a sleek black Cadillac SUV and headed to Kennywood, where his sister Melissa used to work. On the way, as he got off on driving the eighty-thousand-dollar vehicle, he told Sandy that in high school, he always had the hots for the teenyboppers in hot pants who roamed all over the park, smiling and laughing, showing off their perky young tits and tight young legs and asses—but none of them would give him the time of day. He admitted to Sandy that he used to masturbate just looking at "all the young chickies," picturing himself doing things to them with his dick or his tongue while ogling them from a park bench and slyly rubbing his erect penis inside his jeans with a box of popcorn in his lap to cover up what he was doing.

Sandy didn't act like any of his desires were sick or repulsive. She just said, "Nothing sexual turns me off, no matter how weird or nasty. Whatever floats your boat, as far as I'm concerned. When I was in the Navy I actually felt sorry for this one horny sailor because he was ugly as sin and could never get laid, so he'd sit in a porno theater with an empty popcorn box in his lap and his dick inside the box so he could stroke it without anybody being wise to what he was doing. Or at least that's what he hoped. But one day, an usher caught him and threw him out. Lucky for him, the usher didn't call the cops."

"Did he eat the popcorn first before he stuck his dick in?" Bradley asked.

They both laughed.

"I think he kept some of the popcorn *in* there," said Sandy. "Because it felt so nice and warm on his thing, and the butter did a fine job of greasing his hand."

"Damn! That kinda turns me on!" Bradley said.

He wished he could be like Jeffrey Epstein, living the libertine life in high style for sixty-six years before hanging himself in prison. To Bradley, it was worth it to live that long, screwing hordes of luscious young girls, even if you had to die in the end. Hanging was quick— even quicker than an orgasm. As a matter of fact, hanging could *produce* an orgasm; at least he had read that somewhere in an article that claimed that a lot of hanging or strangling victims died with a hard-on, and some were even found to have ejaculated.

"What's gonna be your alias today?" he asked Sandy. "What should I call you?"

"I think Sandy is okay," she replied. "It's generic enough. Just don't use my last name."

"Okay, then, call me Jeffrey."

"Your idol. Maybe you should call me Jizz."

"Huh?" said Bradley, not getting it.

"Jizz," Sandy explained. "Short for Ghislaine

Maxwell, Jeffrey Epstein's procurer. She did for him what I'm going to do for you today."

"Okay, Jizz," Bradley said, giving her a wink. "We'll call you Jizz Layne."

Sandy said, "I'm sure those young girls liked what they got from Jeffrey, maybe not the sex so much, but surely the money. After all, he must've been an old geezer in their eyes. Ms. Maxwell is a beautiful, charming woman—at least she used to be before she went to jail. She would lurk around a school for young girls in Manhattan which happened to be only a block away from Mr. Epstein's mansion, and she would select the most lovely and vulnerable teenagers and seduce them into Jeffrey's domain. I saw one of those girls on TV, whining about what happened to her as if she didn't like it, especially the hundred-dollar bills that were greasing her palms when she was only fourteen. She said that her father had died, and she was having to drop out of school and get a job at McDonald's, so when Ghislaine took a liking to her, it was like heaven opened up for her and her mother. Ghislaine gave her three hundred dollars and took her to meet Jeffrey for the first time, and he was in a huge bathtub, totally naked, playing with a pair of rubber breasts as if they were a rubber ducky. Then he masturbated while she stood there and watched."

"You're kidding me!" Bradley said, highly shocked.

"You don't believe he masturbated in front of a four-teen-year-old girl?" Sandy asked him.

"No," said Bradley. "I just don't believe he needed to play with a pair of rubber breasts. He had plenty of the real stuff to play with."

"Well, be that as it may, that's what the girl claimed," said Sandy.

"She's a fucking liar, just like my sister!" Jerry said.

"She went running to our mom, saying that I kicked her in her crotch."

"You didn't do that?"

"I did it, but only once. She acted like I did it every day and twice on Sundays. Our mom took Melissa to the doctor, and when he found one little bruise, I got grounded for a month! After that, I never forgot about it. I'd pick on my bratty sister every chance I got, even at Kennywood, after she got a job here. My mom wasn't here to protect her, and when she tried to tell on me, it was my word against hers."

"But you were guilty," Sandy said. "I like that. I like it when guilty people know how to get away with it."

Bradley loved that sort of praise, and he basked in it as they walked through the long pedestrian tunnel that enabled folks to enter the park. When they emerged into bright sunlight and the honky-tonk sounds of the barkers and the rides, he asked Sandy, "How do you see us pulling this thing off? First, we've gotta pick our target. Right?"

"No," she said perfunctorily. "First, we have to set ourselves up. Jeffrey Epstein had a mansion, but we only got a park that we don't own, but it's full of prey for us to hunt. You're not going to do the hunting. I am. So you just have to lie in wait, just like Jeffrey Epstein. Not in a bathtub but on a park bench. But you have to look like you're a wealthy gentleman who's above it all. You're like an alpha lion, the leader of the pack, proud, smug, and lazy, letting his consort do all the work. I'll be your Ghislaine Maxwell. You did it?"

"Yes, yes!" Bradley enthused. "You're gonna bring me a delectable young cutie, and I'll get to do anything I want to her."

"Just don't look overly anxious when I introduce you

to your lovely underage victim, and please don't drool on your expensive duds."

For this occasion, Bradley and Sandy had appropriately costumed themselves. They weren't dressed the same way as most of the other folks in the amusement park; they wanted to appear aloof from all that. Sandy was wearing a blue satin dress, high heels, bracelets and earrings. Bradley was wearing tight black trousers, black patent leather shoes, a black sport coat with brass buttons, and a form-fitting black silk shirt. They wanted to zero in on a lovely young girl of their choice and make her totally star-struck by the flashy way they were dressed and the money they would be flashing.

Bradley said, "I know the perfect bench for me to be sitting on, right across from Noah's Ark."

"Is that a fast ride or a slow ride?" Sandy inquired.

"It's not a ride. It's a walk-through kind of thing," Bradley explained. "It's supposed to be a replica of the actual Ark in the Bible, and it's on top of a fake mountain that's not really very high, made of painted plaster, as if it's stranded on some rocks. It actually *does* rock now and then, thanks to some hidden machinery underneath. When I was a teenager, I'd watch the girls crossing the boat deck, knowing that blasts of air would hit them, making their skirts fly up.

"They'd shriek and try to hold their skirts down, and I'd get some pretty good beaver shots 'cause some of 'em weren't even wearing panties. Noah's Ark was my favorite thing here, and next best was the Olde Mill."

"What was the Olde Mill all about?"

"It was a lot like Noah's Ark because once you were going through the dark passages inside either of them, you'd be hit with strobe lights and loud horn blasts every now and then, especially around the darkest corners, where you'd be hit with gruesome displays, like people getting butchered or torn apart. You had to walk through Noah's Ark, but you went through the Olde Mill in low wooden boats that didn't need to be paddled because they were pulled through by rollers hidden under shallow waterways with lots of twists and turns. My favorite display in the Olde Mill was Bloody Mary getting guillotined. It was all done with mannequins, of course, but I could let my imagination take over. There was a masked and hooded executioner dummy with his hand on a big wooden lever, and a dummy of Queen Mary with her spinal cord protruding from her neck and her head lying beside a wicker basket, and the guillotine blade was streaked with her blood. It made me want to see something like that in real life. If I had lived back then, I'd have looked forward to the public executions, no doubt in my mind. I even caught a stray cat and a couple of rabbits now and then and chopped their heads off."

"Damn, Bradley!" Sandy yelped. "You were a serial killer in the making, even as a young boy! Did you have any inkling of that?"

"Not really. I knew I had bizarre thoughts, but I kept them to myself."

"Pretty sneaky," Sandy said.

"Just like *you*," Bradley shot back at her. "The other great thing about the Olde Mill was that the passages were pitch dark except for when the displays leaped out of the darkness. So I'd go through over and over, always hoping to get lucky enough to grab a seat beside some pretty girl going through by herself. I'd pretend to be really scared so I could throw myself up against her and grab feels."

Thinking all this over for a while, Sandy said, "Well, look, Bradley, we aren't rich enough to give you everything you'd like. We can't set you up in a mansion in Manhattan, and we can't buy you a tropical island resort with an airplane to fly rich friends and corrupt politicians back and forth so they can screw young women. You're going to be a pale imitation of your hero, Jeffrey Epstein, but you'll be able to satisfy some of your whimsical erotic appetites, just like he did."

"That's good enough for me," Bradley said. "Matter of fact, it's perfect."

"That must be Noah's Ark," Sandy surmised, looking upward at a semblance of a rickety old-time houseboat rocking on top of fake plaster boulders as if it were rocking on a gigantic hidden seesaw.

"That's it, Sandy! Looks just like I remember it."

She guessed that the mechanisms for causing the Ark to sway back and forth were hidden inside the phony boulders. "Well, pick a bench and start trying to look bored and prosperous," she told Bradley. "And when I fetch some pretty young thing over to you, remember you're Jeffrey, and I'm Jizz."

"Do you think somebody will catch on?"

"To the Jizz Laine thing? Hell, no. Who's going to be thinking in those terms except you and me? Most of these teenyboppers don't watch CNN or MSNBC, so they wouldn't know shit about Jeffrey and Ghislaine. Bye-bye, see you later. I'm going to pick a place to hang out."

Sandy decided to lurk on a bench near the cotton candy concession, where a bevy of teenyboppers was lining up to buy the soft sugary junk. Some of them were fat, and some were thin, but there were quite a few who hadn't lost their bicycle-pumping muscles and still had the kind of trim, shapely bodies that might not last much past adolescence but for now, were great to look at. Superb, in fact. Sandy was hoping to zero in on a hot young thing who was on her own, at least temporarily, without the nuisance of a boyfriend hanging around her or a flighty gaggle of females her own age.

Finally an absolutely stunning young blonde in a pink halter and pink hot pants peeled off from her less attractive girlfriend, saying, "No, don't buy me any cotton candy, Marsha, I *hate* that yicky-sticky sweet stuff. I'll text you later after I hook up with Jimmy in the Penny Arcade."

Sandy slinked across the fairway and confronted the gorgeous girl in mid-stride.

The girl stopped, stared, got miffed, and said, "Excuse me. Why are you blocking my way?"

"My god!" Sandy exclaimed. "Do you realize how beautiful you are?"

"Who're you?" the girl blurted with mild annoyance. "Do I know you from somewhere?"

"I don't think so. But I hope to get to know *you,* honey. I'm a talent scout for a modeling agency. A top agency with a stable of starlets. My name is Jizz Layne."

Sandy offered her bejeweled hand, and the beguiling young woman hesitantly took it.

"I'm here at the park with my director, Jeff Bradley, one of the best in the business. In fact, he just finished a film shoot for Pepsi, and we're just unwinding a bit, plus looking around, hoping to spot fresh young talent like you. May I ask your name?"

"It's Allison. But what makes you think I'm so special...uh...Jizz?"

"Yes, it's Jizz—that's my nickname. Oops! I'm afraid I'm out of business cards, dear. Everybody at the film shoot wanted one. Not everyone gets to be one of our clients, but they all hope to be chosen. You may not realize how lucky you are."

"Well, is there any way I can get in touch with you tomorrow somehow? I have to meet Jimmy—my boyfriend—at the Penny Arcade."

"How's about if I walk you over there, and you can meet Jeffrey on the way? He's in the vicinity of Noah's Ark, and that's not far from the Arcade. Maybe your boyfriend can meet him, too, if you want to bring him over."

"Well...okay...that sounds good, I suppose," Allison mumbled uncertainly.

Sandy was pretty well satisfied that Allison had taken the bait and would soon be reeled in hook, line, and sinker.

Tactfully, and hopefully not being too pushy, Sandy said, "You shouldn't miss this grand opportunity, Allison. It's going to change your life. Unless he's the crazy jealous type, Jimmy will be rooting for you to grab the brass ring."

Brass, not gold. Utterly fake. Sandy allowed herself an inward smirk.

Suddenly somebody was calling out, "Ali! I've been waiting for you! What're you doing?"

Bradley, Sandy, and Allison all turned to look. It was a teenage boy taking rapid strides toward them, then stopping short. He was skinny to the point of gawkiness. His brownish hair looked so dry and brittle that he might have dandruff, and he had more than a few pimples on his chin and the sides of his mouth.

He looked angry, and Allison looked cowed.

Sandy eyed him with disdain.

"Do you take orders from this geek?" Bradley said to Allison.

He had sour memories of his high school days when

some of the brainiacs scored with the chicks better than he did, even though he played football.

With a sneer on his face, Jimmy said, "What the *hell*, Alli?"

"I'm sorry, Jimmy," she said sheepishly. "These people are TV producers, and they want me to do a screen test."

"Bullshit! Don't fall for that crap!" Jimmy said scornfully.

"Please don't insult us," Sandy told him.

"I've been talking with them," Allison interjected, "and I think they are who they say they are."

"And you're a gullible airhead!" said Jimmy.

Bradley decided that he knew just what to say to this smart-assed kid. "Listen, Jimmy," he said cajolingly. "We're going to take Allison to our studio and pay her three hundred dollars so we can take some test photos and she can sign a letter of intent. We'd be happy to pay you another three hundred dollars as her temporary agent or manager."

"You really shouldn't stand in the way of her golden opportunity," Sandy added. "Most models would give just about anything to meet Jeffrey Bradley. He's legendary in his field. And I'm his executive assistant, Jizz Layne."

"I'm pleased to meet you," Jimmy acknowledged. "But I'm not going to be just a temporary agent. Right, Allison?"

She nodded uncertainly.

Jimmy's greediness had been set in motion by the appeal of money and perhaps fame, and the rest was fairly easy. After friendlier words than the ones they started out with, Jimmy and Allison gave in and accompanied "Jizz" and "Jeffrey" to their shiny black Cadillac

SUV in the vast Kennywood parking lot, where all the vehicle slots were crammed full. Which was perfect. A perfect place for Bradley to grab the same knife he had used on his wife from under the car seat, grab Jimmy by his ponytail and slice his throat. Then when the boy fell, gushing blood, he jumped on him and stabbed him over and over, in a mad frenzy, at least six or seven times.

Allison screamed and tried to run—but Sandy, who still possessed strong muscles from working on her hog farm, grabbed the fifteen-year-old girl in a vise-like bear hug while Bradley used zip ties on her wrists and ankles and sealed her mouth shut with duct tape.

"Easy, girl, you're in for a good time," he murmured to her. Then he and Sandy pushed her into the cargo bay of the Cadillac SUV and used the remote to make the back door descend and close.

Bradley kicked Jimmy's bloody body under a nearby pickup truck. Then he got behind the wheel and Sandy got into the front passenger seat.

"You're covered in that boy's blood," Sandy grumbled. "Why the hell did you have to go wild on him? This Caddy is going to need cleaned before we can turn it in, and we certainly can't take it to a car wash."

"Yes we can," Bradley contradicted. "I can take it to one that's self-serve."

"Nobody better see you scrubbing it out," Sandy said. "I'm not helping. It's on you."

"I'll handle it," Bradley said. Then he backed the SUV out of its slot, and they were on their way.

He smiled and laughed, already picturing all the "fun" he was going to have once Allison was naked with him back at the hog farm, where no one would hear her, no matter how loudly she might scream. He could barely wait. First he would strip and burn all of his expensive duds. Then he'd pay her an intimate visit.

He was driving so fast that several times Sandy had to tell him to slow down or else they might get pulled over by a cop.

20

At age five, Melissa relished her big brother's protection. When a bully her same age, a boy bigger than her but much smaller than Bradley, pushed her down, pinned her arms with his bare knees, and made her eat dirt by shoving it into her mouth and squeezing her face as hard as he could to keep her mouth open, Bradley tackled the bully, jumped on top of him and beat his face as hard as he could with both fists. He gave the bully two black eyes and broke two of his front teeth, and the jagged stumps of the teeth cut into his lips and tongue, making blood pour over his chin and onto his white T-shirt.

As she spit black dirt out of her mouth, even as she was scared and appalled by her brother's eruption into such a vicious rage, at the same time, she was pleased by it because she knew that the bully would never attack her again, and neither would any of his pals.

She didn't know that her own big brother, her erstwhile protector, would soon become worse than any of *them*.

One day Bumps, her pet frog, whom she had studied and written about for her fifth-grade science project, seemed to be nowhere in the whole house—until she found it under a chair in the living room—and it was dead, its little head flat-looking and bloody. Bradley admitted he had been playing with Bumps but swore he had put him back on top of the colored pebbles in his glass home. He said that maybe the cat had snatched Bumps somehow, but the more Melissa thought about it, she did not believe it because it had never happened before.

Then something worse happened, about a month or two later, when Bradley got hold of Babsy, a poor little kitten that Melissa had nursed back to health after bringing her home as a stray, sick, and starved. She saw Bradley from her bedroom window, out in the backyard by himself, tying a cord around Bobsy's neck—and she ran out screaming and made him stop. It was one of the rare times that he got grounded. He left Bobsy alone after that, but he turned his rage on Melissa. He mutated from her protector into her worst enemy.

A few months prior to that scary incident, their father had left them and their mother and they were both suffering from the abandonment that had turned them into near orphans, which may have been the thing that turned Bradley crazier. Their mother was now a single mom with two children to finish raising on low-income jobs such as clerking at convenience stores. She succumbed to an alcohol habit but could not afford the expensive stuff, so her poison of choice was sweet, cheap wine by the quart. One of them, her favorite, was called Thunderbird, and every time she got paid, she lined three bottles up on the window ledge. They fortified her for her weekend binges, which she indulged in for about three years—till she was diagnosed with diabetes and at the same time was indoctrinated into a Bible-thumping cult-like church that turned her into a hardened Christian even as it got her into weekly AA meetings in the church basement.

The upshot was that she got sober and stayed that way, up till now, but she was never much of a warm, loving mother to Melissa because Bradley was her hands-down favorite and could do no wrong in her eyes, and she made no bones about it. She spoiled her son rotten and aided and abetted his cruelty toward her daughter, Melissa, and treated Melissa like a third wheel, good for dusting, vacuuming, washing clothes, and doing dishes—which she was doing that day when Bradley sneaked up behind her and kicked her between her legs.

Due to her brother's abuse, Melissa suffered from nightmares and flashbacks without getting any help dealing with them. She became a lonely, frightened child with no close friends to confide in—because she could not bring herself to trust anyone.

Her deep-seated fears, rational and irrational, mushroomed all the way through grade school and into seventh grade. Then, one day while riding her bicycle—a banged-up boy's bike that used to be Bradley's—she met a girl who became her best friend and secret idol—Sherry Bartley. Sherry was in the same grade as Melissa but not in the same homeroom or in any of her same classes. But Sherry was one of the "cool girls"—a cheerleader and a member of the swimming team—while Melissa was on the outside looking in, except she was always on the Honor Roll, and Sherry wasn't.

To Melissa, it was a wonder and somewhat of a miracle that a blonde, beautiful, and athletic cool kid like Sherry liked her so much that she wanted to be her friend. And Sherry's family was cool, too. Her father was a police detective and her mother was an English teacher —and they treated Melissa much better than she ever got treated at home. Many times George Bartley would say, "If you were an orphan, Melissa, I would adopt you." This made Melissa blush with a sense of pride that she had seldom felt before.

George Bartley's favorite thing was to hold cook-outs in the Bartley backyard, where he and some of his cop friends had built a large picnic shelter, a barbecue pit, and an in-ground swimming pool—and Melissa was always invited to the cook-outs, and she absolutely loved being made welcome and being allowed to hear "cop talk" between George and his colleagues.

For her, it was a revealing, enlightening exposure to how wonderful real friends and family could be. And it had the surprising effect of starting to bring her out of her shell, in a place and a situation where she wasn't under the dark threat of her brother's presence.

Her budding awareness of her own self-worth was heightened when Sherry's father enlisted her to help bring Sherry's grades up. Sherry's mom, Carla, said, "My own daughter doesn't want me to tutor her in theme writing and her book reports for her English and history classes, but she'll accept tutoring from you, Melissa, so you're it, like it or not. We'll even pay you like we would a babysitter." But Melissa insisted she'd do it for nothing.

During her time with the Bartleys, which without question was the best time of Melissa's young life, her exposure to smatterings of insider talk about the cases worked on by Detective George Bartley and his pals started to move her in that direction when she had to start thinking about a career. In the absence of a "father image" in her own home, Sherry's father somewhat filled that role, and Melissa had him on a pedestal that influenced her toward law enforcement. But rather than aspiring toward being on a small-town police force, she began to research the FBI's role in solving interstate kidnappings and murders and, especially, fighting home-grown terrorism.

She thought that if she could belong to something bigger than herself, she might realize her own potential and thus conquer or at least partly subdue the inner demons that were spawned by her own brother and continued to haunt her.

21

Vince and Melissa were engaging in intense foreplay, breathing hard with their hands all over each other—until she froze and rolled away from him, crying inconsolably. He tried to pull her close to him again, but she resisted so strongly that her body went rigid.

He didn't understand what was happening. He reached out to touch her, but she jerked away from him with a tiny distraught gasp. He didn't know what to do, so he let her cry while he tried to deal with being rejected in such a hurtful way.

Eventually she started talking softly, the words tumbling out while she still faced away from him. She made Vince realize that the abuse by her brother went beyond the other sexual aggressions that she had described or alluded to. Even now, she didn't get more specific about certain aspects, but she admitted that she had been traumatized in such a way that she was terrified by thoughts of having sex with anyone.

She said, "I'm in love with you, Vince. At least I think

I am or could be, but maybe I don't deserve you. I'm damaged goods. I wouldn't blame you if you walked away from me."

Tenderly he told her, "You're not going to easily kill what I feel for you."

More tears came as she turned toward him.

Even as he desperately wanted to comfort her, he was wrestling with his new awareness that even though she was a highly educated, no-nonsense professional woman on the surface, inwardly, she obviously was suffering great torment.

Once again, he risked touching her, and she didn't brush his hand aside.

Words started tumbling out of her. She said that she had never gotten any sort of treatment for anxiety or depression and had never sought counseling because she knew that once that kind of thing went into her medical records her chance of ever becoming an FBI agent would be gone forever.

He gently asked, "Does that mean you've never had any kind of counseling?"

"I went to several group therapy sessions offered by the Pittsburgh YWCA after I found out that I needn't state my identity, I could be there anonymously. I was still scared to go, but I forced myself."

"Let's talk some more," Vince said. "I'm in no hurry to go. But can I have some coffee?"

He wanted to get her busy with something normal, something unthreatening.

They talked till the wee hours, even though they both had pressing obligations for the following morning, but Vince thought that now wasn't the time to worry about being sleep-deprived. He cared too much about Melissa to even think of deserting her. But after that, he couldn't get thoughts of what had happened to her out of his mind. For the next few days, in the midst of his worries about her, he had moments where he wanted to hunt down her own brother and make sure he wasn't brought in alive, but that was a fantasy he knew he couldn't carry out.

He wanted to learn more about ways he might help her. He didn't trust his ability to handle the situation wisely or even delicately enough. He wondered who he might talk to about that without necessarily letting her know. He wanted to know what the role of a spouse or a significant other ought to be when the woman he loved was raped or abused.

He decided that he should do some research on his own before consulting anyone in person. Because he was a detective in the major crimes unit of the Allegheny County Sheriff's Office, he already knew that one in four women would be sexually assaulted in their lifetimes. But now, that appalling statistic had become personal.

He went online and plugged in: How should a man help his spouse or girlfriend who has been sexually abused? He clicked on an article that started out by saying that survivors "often face rocky terrain when it comes to reclaiming sex or romance after being harmed." Well, that's obvious, he thought to himself, while going on to read that the specific challenges could include the inability to get aroused, lack of interest in sex, inability to experience pleasure, or even an urge to seek out sexual engagements that were high risk.

Vince thought that the inability to get aroused could be crossed off because, in his opinion, both he and Melissa had been pretty far along in the arousal department before she broke it off. He read that the partner should affirm the survivor's experience, accept the current boundaries of the relationship and demonstrate a willingness to be patient. However, the most well-meaning partner could not heal a survivor's trauma. Sincere, deeply felt assurances and steadfast support could help immensely, but the survivor herself would have to win the battle over her inner struggle.

Another article, consisting of personal accounts of ways in which abused women were left suffering, quoted a woman who said, "My two assaults have left me completely scarred. The first time I had consensual sex, I cried for the next thirty-six hours."

Stunned by this and by several other admissions quoted in the article, Vince decided that he should seek advice from the psychologist employed by the county police department to offer counseling to cops suffering emotional problems, including those following incidents involving shootings while on duty. Without hesitation, Dr. Pomeroy agreed to talk to Vince in his private office in Pittsburgh's upscale Shadyside section.

Dr. Pomeroy wore gray trousers, gray suspenders, and a dark-gray necktie, his gray suit jacket draped over his chair as he sat behind his large mahogany desk. His hair was thick and not totally gray, with still some brown in it, and he wore fashionable glasses with discreetly small black frames.

Sitting on a couch against the opposite wall, Vince related the details of what had transpired between him and Melissa in her bedroom, and after mulling it over, the doctor said, "I always hesitate to say that a woman ever totally gets over a sexual assault, but I believe that disclosing what she's been through is an important first step. She must care a lot about you to have done that."

"I think she does," Vince admitted. "And I think she's the best thing that has ever happened to me."

"Or could be," Dr. Pomeroy cautioned. "If she can pull herself together enough. Otherwise, you're in for a hell of a ride."

"You don't sound too hopeful."

"I just want you to fully understand what you may be taking on here. Navigating intimacy after deep affliction is particularly challenging due to how our brains store trauma. We're hard-wired to hang onto our more fearful experiences than our happier times. It's a self-protective mechanism that warns us to painstakingly avoid any situation that might mirror the ones we've hated most. Our brain sometimes also has trouble differentiating between whether the trauma is happening right now or in the past."

"You mean like flashbacks?" Vince said.

"Yes. Sort of," said Dr. Pomeroy. "It's as if the mere idea of having consensual sex becomes identified with the horrors already lived through. In other words, the sufferer comes to deeply believe, subconsciously or even consciously, that any form of sex must always be feared. It can be a self-inflicted prison, a torment that the sufferer can never escape."

Vince left his meeting with Dr. Pomeroy in great doubt over his ability to help Melissa cope with her demons. But he knew that he had to stick with her. She had already taken the very difficult step of opening up to him, and that awareness gave him hope that she might open up more. Still, he wanted to be her lover and her lifelong partner more than he wanted to be her savior, a role that might be the antithesis of love. He didn't want her kneeling at his feet in some kind of gratitude; he wanted her to be upright, by his side, going through the rest of their lives together as equals. Equals in fortitude as well as affection. He believed that he could love Melissa deeply enough to achieve that and to deserve it.

And that was something new to him.

As a callow young man, he had cavalierly played the field, at times having two or three girlfriends at the same time and keeping them blissfully unaware and apart from one another. But when he got caught, it was devastating for all concerned. After that, he eventually dared to enter into a relationship in which he vowed to behave more honorably and to cherish just one woman. But once again, he had faltered, and he got his comeuppance when she broke off their engagement and told him she never wanted to see him again. Ever since then, although he had been with a few different women, he had always made it clear from the outset that he wasn't looking for anything permanent. And so his own lack of commitment had doomed those relationships from the start, which he belatedly realized. He had always kept a secret part of himself too aloof and too cold.

Right now, at this more mature stage of his life, he was ready to be loved. Perhaps with Melissa, he didn't really have a chance. But he was going to offer her the best of himself and hope that he might help her heal, even if he lost her in the process. He recognized the changes and uncertainties they would both have to go through. But he was determined to try.

22

On Tuesday morning, the day after Vince Spivak's talk with Dr. Pomeroy, he and Jerry Delaney were sipping large black coffee to jump-start themselves into another tough day with murder investigations that seemed to be going nowhere. They were both morose.

Needing a break from his dismal thoughts, Jerry asked, "How're things going with you and Melissa?"

Vince shrugged as if there was a problem he wasn't ready to talk about, and Jerry was about to back off, but then his cell phone rang, and he tugged it out of his pocket and listened.

"Well, that's something," he said into the phone. "Too bad they didn't get a CODIS hit though."

He listened a half-minute longer, then put his cell phone back in his pocket.

Vince said, "Was that Sheriff Patton? You perked up like it was good news."

"Sort of," Jerry told him bemusedly. "The CSI people got two DNA samples from the lamp fragments at the Warner's house. One was the wife's, and the other presumably was the killer's because it turned out to match the male DNA at the Jackie Kelter crime scene. If her husband killed *her*, he also must've helped murder the Warners. But *if* it was him, his DNA wasn't in the CODIS system because he has no criminal record—which of course we already knew. But now it looks like he's turned into a spree killer."

Vince said, "Bradley Kelter is still our prime suspect, but something has caused him to accelerate. I have a feeling he's teamed up with somebody just as psychotic as he is, or maybe worse. Somebody who's egging him on."

"Madness for two," Jerry said, grimacing pedantically. "That's the phrase that was coined back in the eighteen-hundreds by criminalists in Paris. I don't know to pronounce it right, but in French, it's called *folie à deux*, their term for describing a weird phenomenon that can result when two or more people with borderline antiso-cial tendencies, or borderline psychosis, manage to latch on to each other as house-mates, partners, close associates or especially as lovers. The Manson Family is a prime example, isolated on a ranch in the desert and succumbing to their own delusions. Or the Hillside Strangler in Los Angeles, which turned out to be *two* people instead of one, two demented cousins working together, wallowing in their crimes and aiding and abet-ting each other's madness."

"Yeah, I knew that about the stranglers," Vince said. "They raped and killed young women and dumped their bodies on the hills above the highways."

"We might be dealing with something similar," Jerry said ruefully. "It sure seems like Bradley Kelter has teamed up with somebody who's maybe worse than he is. We just don't know who."

23

Z ip-tied and utterly terrified, her mouth sealed with duct tape, Allison Cisneros suffered a long, heart-wrenching ride sprawled on her side and bouncing around in the cargo bay of her captors' Cadillac SUV. For the first part of the ordeal, they mostly seemed to be on a high-speed highway, perhaps Route 30 or the Pennsylvania Turnpike, but after that, she felt the twists and turns of the vehicle's maneuverings, and then it got bumpier and seemingly a lot slower, till it finally stopped.

The cargo door opened and the dapper but evil man who had called himself Jeffrey Bradley stood there with a knife. The blade glinted in the sun as it went toward her, and she cowered away from it even though there was nowhere for her to go. The blade continued coming at her, suddenly not toward her face but toward her ankles, and the zip ties that bound them together were suddenly severed.

Menacing her with his knife, the man said, "Get out, Allison!"

He pulled on her left ankle, then on the zip-tie around her wrists, making her jump down from the van. The woman who had called herself Jizz Layne slammed the cargo door shut, and she and "Jeffrey" forced Allison up onto the porch and into the house and then up a dark, rickety flight of stairs and into a room where she was pushed down onto a mattress and tied down with rope, securing her to brass bed rungs.

Through all this, she kept envisioning the horrific way that her boyfriend, Jimmy Cardoza, was shot and killed. He wasn't a jock, and she wasn't a majorette or a cheerleader. He wasn't picked on in school and wasn't considered a geek, just a quiet kind of kid who liked to draw in charcoal and paint in oils and watercolors. She wasn't one of the so-called "cool kids" either. She shared his fascination with art and music, not punk rock or heavy metal but the older stuff their classmates thought was at best terribly ancient and out of style, songs by Frank Sinatra, Tony Bennett, and the like. Jimmy and Allison had kept what their schoolmates would consider "far-out tastes" mostly to themselves because they didn't want to be called "different."

Allison had never thought of herself as beautiful, but she had dared to hope that she was when Jizz Layne had told her so. Now she inwardly cursed her susceptibility to flattery. It got Jimmy killed and herself into a weird kind of captivity. With utter dismay, she realized that at the very least she was going to be raped, and she prayed that her ordeal would end there—but doubted that it would. As she was being forced into the old, foreboding farmhouse, she feared that she might be held there as a sex slave or, even worse, that she might not be held there but sold to sex or dope traffickers in Mexico.

She didn't dare to hope that she was going to be

ransomed, because her mother and father didn't have any substantial money. Would friends, neighbors, or even some public benefactor step up to pay her kidnappers if money was all they were after? Would somebody start a GoFundMe page? The prospect of that kind of help in her dire situation seemed totally farfetched. Her father, just like Jimmy's father, had lost his job during the worst part of the Covid epidemic. They both had low-level jobs to begin with and now they were working as convenience store clerks in two different strip malls where they got paid less than minimum wage. It seemed as if their old high-paying jobs were never coming back. To try to make ends meet, Allison's mom was working at a Salvation Army store.

The more that these factors tumbled through her mind, the more hopeless she felt. It was likely that at this point nobody knew that she had been captured and Jimmy had been killed. Even if his body were discovered when it got dark, and Kennywood closed down and the parking lot emptied of vehicles, Allison couldn't imagine that the kidnappers had left the sort of clues that might lead to her rescue. Her parents might become alarmed when she failed to come home tonight, but until then they would assume she was still with her boyfriend, having fun.

She felt as if she must be in the middle of nowhere. She wondered what could possibly lead the police or anybody else to where she was being kept prisoner. She worried that they might not keep looking for her after they hit a dead end. If they killed her and buried her out here, her case would probably go cold and her body would never be found.

The woman she knew as Jizz Layne suddenly came into the room and stared at her for a long while. She came closer, bent down and tugged at the ropes that secured Allison to the brass bed rungs, then said contemplatively, "Bradley could've used zip ties, I guess, but these ropes are pretty secure. I suppose he wants the option of loosening the ropes depending upon what he wishes to make you do for him."

She stood up, smiled, then harshly ripped the duct tape from Allison's mouth. "We don't need to keep your snotty mouth taped shut any more because there's nobody anywhere near this place who could hear you scream. So you should just accept your situation and make up your mind to be nice. You're going to be a sex toy for Bradley, so you might as well get used to it."

Allison started crying and trembling, pulling on the ropes as hard as she could, making the bed shake—all to no avail.

"Jizz Layne" laughed at her.

It was a coarse, mocking, almost demonic kind of laugh, almost like the ones inside the Noah's Ark funhouse.

When Jizz Layne sashayed out of Allison's shabby bedroom prison, Allison tried to pray but could not. But the mental block had little to do with the trauma she was suffering and much more to do with the fact that even before these sorry circumstances had engulfed her, she had been painfully rebelling against her Catholic religion. And so was her boyfriend, Jimmy, before he was viciously murdered. She was troubled by the church's teaching that if Jimmy had not been in a state of grace when he died, he would right now be burning forever in hell. And she knew for a fact that he was not in a state of grace, for yesterday, they had gone all the way for their very first time.

They both came from large second-generation families, originally from Mexico, and their homes were permeated with religious fervor. In their kitchens and in every bedroom were the iconic symbols of their ancient Catholicism, including crucifixes, rosary beads, and framed prints of the Bleeding Heart of Jesus. Taking the first tentative steps toward becoming a disbeliever was a fearsome, almost an earth-shaking thing. Allison and Jimmy didn't dare let any of their friends or family members know that they were having "heretical thoughts." They had been raised as "good Catholics," never missing Mass on Sundays or Holy Days and submitting to confession, Holy Communion, and Confirmation in the prescribed sequences. They knew that if their questioning of religion got out, they would be thought of as heathens, and their families would be utterly disgraced. They might even be cast out. And so they needed to keep their mouths shut about their newfound beliefs and their need for exploration of different ways of thought. If someday they should want to marry, as a part of their benumbed silence, they would need to go through with a church wedding. They would need to pretend that they still adhered to all the rituals, taking marriage instructions from a priest who was presumably celibate and outwardly respecting all the doctrines that they were raised to believe in, mumbling the prayers as always and forever and not letting on that they had lapsed.

Even before she had been kidnapped, Allison had been dealing with all these fears, plus the secret hovering fear of being pregnant. She had lain with Jimmy without using any birth control. And so now, in addition to the possibility that she was going to be repeatedly raped and then killed, she was frightened that she might be pregnant, and without any way of knowing for sure.

A desperate thought struck her. What if she told her captors that she *was* pregnant, never mind whether it was true or not? Would that elicit enough sympathy from them that they would let her go free? But she immediately knew that it wouldn't, because they were obviously too cruel and heartless. They would sooner murder her and bury her in the woods.

Out of complete and futile desperation, she tried to regress into the old religious beliefs that she and Jimmy had been discarding. She forced herself to recite an Act of Contrition, but she was unable to get very far into it. "Oh my god, I am heartily sorry for having offended Thee, and I renounce all my sins because I dread the loss of heaven and the pains of hell…"

That was as far as she got. The rest of the words wouldn't come. Instead came tears. Great wrenching sobs that racked her entire body. The spasms caused the ropes to cut into her ankles and wrists, and twisting sideways, she saw drops of her own blood on the plastic-encased mattress.

Then the people she knew as Jeffrey and Jizz came into the room.

They shook their heads sadly, looking down at her in pity and disapproval, as if she had misbehaved.

Jeffrey was naked, and he had an erection. And now Allison was more scared than ever before.

24

Jimmy Cardoza's bloody body was found after Kennywood closed, and Sheriff Patton, Vince Spivak and Jerry Delaney were on the scene. Two uniformed deputies were stringing plastic yellow-and-black crime scene tape around a tight area that encompassed the body and was hemmed in by orange traffic cones.

Sheriff Patton said, "This is one more case of overkill. The number of times the victim was stabbed shows we've got the same psychopathic trademark as with Jackie Kelter and the Warners. The killer's M.O. makes it look like the cases must be connected. But how?"

Jerry asked, "Was there any ID on the vic?"

"We have his wallet. His name is Jimmy Cardoza, only fifteen years old. Just starting his life, and now it's over."

Vince said, "If Bradley Kelter did this, it's somewhat of a departure. He likes it best when he's stabbing women. Not boys."

"Well, shit," Sheriff Patton said. "We don't know that

this kid wasn't with a girlfriend, maybe. We might find out when we question his parents. Damn! I hate having to break it to them."

"Let me and Vince handle it," Jerry said. "Our first move, considering that there might be a connection to our other cases, is obviously to interview the boy's parents. Believe me, I'm not looking forward to it, but it has to be done. Then we'll follow up on any leads that develop from there, and we'll keep you in the loop."

"Gotcha," the sheriff said. "We'll have each other's back."

"I can't stand working these kinds of cases," Vince said. "They almost make me wish I was fifteen years younger and still handing out speeding tickets."

"Or walking a beat and fifteen pounds lighter," Jerry said, then added, "Sorry, I'm not trying to be funny."

"I understand," said the sheriff. "We all need to distract ourselves from the bad shit we have to deal with."

But over the next five weeks, the investigation into Jimmy Cardoza's murder and the apparent kidnapping of Allison Cisneros went nowhere, just like the other two murder investigations on Vince and Jerry's plate. They had quickly found out that Jimmy's girlfriend, Allison, had been with him at Kennywood, but there had been no trace of her after that. No one had spotted her leaving the park. But she was gone. Presumed dead.

Jerry's mom had passed away in the meantime, and the funeral had taken place two weeks ago. He was still grieving but trying to cheer up in front of his wife and children. One morning over coffee and doughnuts before the start of their shift, he had ventured to ask Vince how things were going between him and Melissa. "You gonna marry that gal or what?" he had said jokingly.

"We're dealing with some issues," Vince admitted.

Jerry didn't ask what kind of issues, he just kept his mouth shut and waited for Vince to say more if he wished to do so. And finally Vince took a deep breath and said, "We're both in a therapy group that keeps everything confidential, no paperwork, no forms to submit anywhere. We pay in the form of donations, whatever we can afford whenever we want to pay it."

"Why're you *both* in therapy?" Jerry dared to ask.

Vince took another deep breath and told Jerry not to say a word about it to anybody, but Melissa's abuse by her fugitive brother had gone deeper than he and Jerry at first knew. He added some details, but not many, then said, "I'm going to the sessions with her to support her all I can. She's making progress…but so am I. I'm not the male chauvinist pig that I used to be. I love her, and I hope we'll eventually get married. Will you be my best man?"

"I'd be honored," Jerry said. "And if I can help in any way in the meantime, please let me know. Otherwise, I'll keep my nose out of it. And I won't tell anyone, not even Jenny."

"Thanks, partner," Vince said with a smile of relief. "I should've opened up to you a lot sooner. Melissa likes Jenny and your kids a whole lot. Maybe your wife can be Melissa's maid of honor."

"I'm sure she'll say yes to that," Jerry said. "In fact, I'm sure she'll be flattered."

25

S andy Jacobs was in a post-op conference with Dr. Heller, sitting directly in front of him while he sat behind his desk. For the past two and a half months, television coverage about the missing teenage girl, Allison Cisneros, had been frantic and intense, with very little let-up, as always happened when a victim happened to be young, white, female and beautiful. Sandy had to push it out of her mind to concentrate on her own healing and her own future. During the weeks that she had been recovering from her operation, she had told herself again and again that she and Bradley weren't in imminent danger. In fact they were probably not in any danger at all. It was highly unlikely that they would ever get caught.

Going over the unfolding of the murder and kidnapping, Sandy couldn't see any flaws in the way they had pulled it off. No witnesses in the parking lot. No give-aways to their true identities even when they made contact with Allison and Jimmy, because the necessary contact at the most had lasted only ten or twelve minutes until they all headed to the rented Cadillac SUV. A few other teenagers may have observed Allison or Jimmy talking to strangers before leaving Kennywood, and if so, they could describe the strangers, but so what. There was nothing to directly connect fictitious "Jizz" and "Jeffrey" to their victims, one still alive and one dead.

Pushing all these considerations aside for the time being, Sandy gave her undivided attention to Dr. Heller, pleased by the way he was now looking at her, seemingly finding her quite attractive. Appraising herself in a full-length mirror before she left to come here, she was gratified to see that, thanks to the hormones she was taking, she was looking even more attractive and feminine than before. She had lightened her shoulder-length hair with shades of light blonde and darker blonde because men thought blondes were sexy and not too bright, which was what she wanted them to think. She was coiffed and made up in a very chic way, so much so that it would be hard for anyone to imagine that she would ever murder anyone.

Dr. Heller said, "I'm glad to tell you that your procedure is a remarkable success and one of my very best efforts. You're no longer a convalescent. You are as good as new, so to speak, a vibrantly attractive woman. You can go forward in life with total confidence. That includes not only relationships but sexual *relations*, if I may be blunt."

"Of course I was going to ask about that," Sandy said.

"I'm sure," the doctor said. "It's a topic that some women are hesitant to broach, but you have always been frank and open-minded, which is the way it should be. The desire for sex is universal and natural, and there is no reason that you need to abstain, but it's only been six weeks post-op, so refrain for two more weeks. I'm pleased that you've retained breast sensitivity, and soon we'll talk about implants."

Sandy said, "I still want to keep my farm—and my animals. Is there any reason for me to stop doing heavy farm work?"

"Not at all. Like any other person, you don't want to do anything that might make you hurt yourself, but otherwise, you're as normal as anyone else. Continue to perform the vaginal dilations that I'm certain you've kept up with because if you weren't, I would have seen signs of at least partial closure. And remember to use lubrication during sex."

"I'm very careful about hygiene."

"That I can tell. You should be very proud of yourself, Sandy. You're going to make some lucky man a fine trophy wife if you should so choose."

"I haven't decided that yet," Sandy said.

As she drove back to the farm after her appointment with Dr. Heller, Sandy felt light-hearted, reborn, brand new in body and soul, and more sure than ever that her male genitals had been a development mistake in her mother's womb. If she had been superstitious, she might have suspected witchcraft. But she respected science, and science had now corrected a genetic blunder. Besides, it was possible for women to rule a world without men, while the reverse of that was impossible. Men did not have wombs; their contribution to the birthing process was only a few drops of semen; it was all pleasure and no pain. But thanks to modern sperm banks, they were no longer needed.

Sandy could not have a child now, but in all other respects, she was female, including in her own mind. As far back as she could remember, she had known that she was a woman who had somehow mistakenly been born into a male body. She was only five years old and outwardly a boy when she began furtively trying on some of her mother's panties and nylons. But when she was fourteen, she got caught at it, and her parents became terribly alarmed that he might be—God forbid —gay. They confronted him about it, and totally mortified, he admitted that he had always felt that he was actually female, even though his genitals said otherwise. This was huge not only for his parents but also for the rigid, dogmatic pastor and Bible-thumping elders of their hell-fire-and-brimstone Born Again church.

The pastor pushed hard for an exorcism, but the Board of Elders considered themselves to be more enlightened than that, in this day and age, and they decreed that the boy, Sandford, should be subjected to sexual identity therapy, and his parents must consent to it, under the threat of excommunication.

On his own, in a wishful attempt to understand himself, Sandy researched his condition on a computer in his small-town library. He learned that there were many other boys who believed, almost from birth, that they were the opposite gender, which was labeled *gender dysphoria* as opposed to *cisgender*, which was the term used for those who identified with the gender that they outwardly appeared to be. Boys like Sandy often started cross-dressing at an early age. They might prefer toys of the opposite gender or prefer playing with girls instead of boys. Some strongly disliked their own genitals and went so far as to attempt or actually succeed in self-mutilation or suicide. But on the other hand, sex aversion therapy sometimes succeeded beautifully, or so it was claimed. One fellow said that his mind had been "washed clean" and he was able to get married and sire three children.

However, most secular mental health experts were of the opinion that it was wrong to pathologize the human condition. Their view was that the wide range of human sexuality should simply be accepted, and none of its manifestations deserved to be stigmatized.

Sandy chose not to kill himself or run away from home but to obey his parents and the church elders. He was sent away to a special church camp for persons with his "problem." He underwent sexual identity therapy, which was sometimes called *conversion therapy*. There was also a more pejorative term for it: *Rainbow Washing*. There were fifteen boys being treated, including himself. It was called the Journey into Manhood Camp. The "worship leader" told them that they should pull their hair out by its roots whenever they had a girlish or homosexual thought. In case their gender crisis was motivated by a deep underlying animosity toward their fathers, they had sessions where they were instructed to pretend that a punching bag was their father and were handed a base-ball bat to pound the hell out of it.

At the end of his six weeks of the so-called Journey into Manhood, Sandy didn't have a feeling that he was "cured," but he made up his mind to pretend otherwise. And as soon as he turned eighteen, he joined the Marine Corps, not so much because it was a masculine pursuit but because he hoped he would see the world and get away from his church, his family, and others who would not accept him as female.

In two of the foreign cities where he was stationed on leave, he murdered a total of five people, two males and three females, for various reasons that he could not readily articulate, but he felt that it had nothing to do with his gender dysphoria except for his rage at those who had tormented him or abused him for it. Be that as it may, he was clever enough never to have been arrested either by civilian or military authorities. He served his twenty years in the Corps, then got out and began collecting a small pension. He used his savings to buy his farm and started taking steps to become the she that he *wanted* to be.

26

S andy got Bradley Kelter out of her way for the better part of a Saturday by sending him on a wild goose chase. She pleaded that she wanted to go with him to rob an elderly couple on a farm near Evans City, but she was too sick to go because she was having adhesions.

"Does that mean your pussy is closing up on you?"

"Watch your mouth!" she snapped at him.

She was sick of him and wanted to be free of him for good. She wanted to be her own woman. She wanted to begin leading her life as a female libertine. She didn't want or need any other encumbrances. But for the time being, she still needed him.

She was fully aware that the farm couple, Hank and Edith Mayfield, didn't really have any goods or money worth stealing. The only "crop" they grew in their fields was pine trees, and they barely eked out a living doing it. They sold the trees in different stages, from sprouting to full grown to landscapers year round, or to purveyors of Christmas trees during the holiday season. Once a year, they would come and buy a hog from Sandy, have it loaded into their rusty old pickup, and take it home to have it butchered and dressed. They were penny pinchers to the core, the old farts, so they made use of every part of each animal they bought, including the hide, which they scraped and tanned, and the feet, which they pickled.

Sandy chuckled inwardly when she gave Bradley instructions and got him primed to rob the husband-and-wife misers, knowing he would end up empty-handed. But she would have plenty of time to deal with Allison Cisneros while he was gone.

After he departed on the mission she had laid out for him, armed with his big knife and her shotgun, Sandy entered the room where Allison was still being kept naked and tied to the brass bed rungs. Bradley had suggested that the two tall curtained windows should be nailed shut or boarded up and the room should be outfitted with a strong steel door instead of the flimsy wooden one so the girl wouldn't have to be tied up most of the time, but Sandy had always said that the expense wasn't worth it because Allison would only be with them for a while longer. Bradley never looked happy when she said that. He was still enjoying her regularly and didn't want to kill her yet, but Sandy had different ideas. She was pretty sure that Bradley had become smitten with the young sexpot, and she was bitterly amused by that and also wary that he might actually decide to free her and help her escape somehow, perhaps by fleeing along with her. And that would mean that he would kill Sandy first, doing unto her before she could do unto him, and for damned sure, Sandy wasn't going to let that happen.

She had employed several degenerates as her handymen before Bradley came along and had killed them each in turn and had fed them to her hogs. Of course she had never mentioned that to Bradley and he had never thought to ask about her previous farm hands, if any, as if it had never occurred to him that she could hardly have run this whole place all by herself every single day. His head was clouded with stupid fantasies, Sandy thought, because he was so damned pussy whipped. He might even be deluded into thinking that he and Allison could go on the lam as man and wife.

Staring down at Allison, Sandy watched her murmuring fitfully in her sleep. With a scornful feeling of superiority, she dwelled on the fact that the young girl wasn't as trim and fit as she was when first brought here. From lack of exercise, fresh air, and sunlight, she was now deathly pale and going flabby. Sandy woke her by untying the rope securing her left wrist, and she groggily stared up at Sandy and said, "I have to pee."

"I'll bring the bedpan," Sandy said.

But instead, she pulled the rope loose from the rungs, threaded it quickly through the small gap between the back of Allison's head and the plastic-covered mattress, then grabbed both ends and yanked it tightly around her neck. When Allison's left hand flailed and clawed at her, Sandy punched the girl as hard as she could three or four times, and her efforts subsided. She groaned and gurgled as Sandy strangled her. It took a long time, but Sandy enjoyed it.

The nice thing about strangling was that it didn't leave any messy bloodstains. Nothing much to clean up, except Allison did wet the plastic covering of the mattress. No big deal because it could be easily sopped up. Sometimes people who were choked to death bled a little from their nostrils, but that didn't happen this time. There were the telltale blood spots in the whites of the eyes, which coroners depended upon to diagnose foul play and turn detectives loose on perpetrators, but of course that didn't need to be worried about on this particular occasion. The purplish rope burns didn't matter either. Nothing mattered to Allison anymore.

For a short while, Sandy stood over her victim, panting from the effort of killing her. Then she spoke to her as if she were still alive and could hear.

"My hogs need to be fed. It's been too long since they've had any of my special human treats. Bradley won't miss you for long, Allison. He'll get over you just fine. He'll soon realize that you're not half the woman that I am. I'm mildly infatuated with him, you see, because we're so much alike. We have the same needs. If we had kept you alive, he probably would have liked a threesome, as perverse as he is, but I can't tolerate the competition, and I've just always been that way. You've served your purpose well up till now, while I was indisposed. And now you've got another special purpose to fulfill for my animals."

———

DETECTIVES Spivak and Delaney were in Jerry's cubicle, taking lids off of their coffee containers and grabbing pastries out of a bag with a famous logo on it.

Vince said, "Why do you keep on going there, Jerry? It's too expensive, and all they have is doughnuts and muffins, way too fattening."

Jerry said, "Comfort food. We need it when we're frustrated."

"Don't you worry about how it clogs your arteries?"

"I figure once I achieve fifty percent blockage, my heart will only have to work half as hard because it'll only have to pump to half of my blood vessels. It's simple math, right?"

"*Simple* is the operative word, that's for certain."

"I tell you something logical, and you make fun of me. I might need a different partner."

With a sigh, Vince said, "We've got four horrific homicides on our hands and possibly a kidnapping, if it's not another killing with the corpse yet to be found. And we're stuck. The cases are going to go permanently cold if we don't catch a break. Any ideas? Or is your brain as clogged as your arteries?"

"Well, photos of Bradley Kelter were all over the news when his wife's murder first broke, but there's been very little media coverage in the past couple of months. I think we ought to put the TV stations to work for us again."

"They'll need us to feed them something fresh. Not just a rehash."

"Maybe can tell them that the Kelter murder and the Kennywood murder and kidnapping are connected."

"Except we're not really sure of that."

"We're pretty sure," Jerry said.

"But not sure enough, and it might blow up in our face," Vince said worriedly. But then, after mulling it over some more, he said, "I understand what you're saying. We don't have anything viable to go, so maybe we should take a shot in the dark."

"Semi-dark," Jerry insisted.

"Okay, semi-dark. Let's do it," Vince decided. "But let's run it by the sheriff first so we don't get fired."

"Getting fired would almost be welcome," said Jerry.

———

THE DOOR to the farmhouse opened, and Sandy came out, awkwardly carrying Allison's corpse, still talking to Allison as if she were still alive.

"Damn it, if I rupture myself carrying you around, it'll be *your* fault. Dr. Heller told me not to strain myself too much, but I've got to feed my hogs while Bradley is on that wild goose I sent him on. Don't worry, he'll get over you. I'll make sure of that when we're in bed together. And if he doesn't let me satisfy him, I'll make him regret it."

When Sandy reached the hog pen, she set Allison's body down so she could open the gate, then picked the body up again and talked to it.

"Bradley would have balked if I'd asked him to help with you. I think he got smitten with you, Allison, which is why I have to do this by myself."

She entered the pen, stooped over by the weight she was carrying, and called out to her hogs.

"Here, sweeties! Come to Mama! I fetched you something you're gonna like!"

She dumped the body into the pen, then re-fastened the gate.

The hogs snuffled and snorted as they gathered around the body and began to tear it apart.

Sandy watched with a smile on her face.

————

THE FARMHOUSE DOOR BANGED OPEN, and Sandy jumped up, wanting to grab her shotgun till she realized it wasn't there in the corner of the kitchen, its usual place.

Bradley came in carrying it, his face all lit up with

glee. In the hand that wasn't holding the shotgun, he held a shopping bag that seemed to be full of something.

"Ha-haw!" he cried out, laughing. "Let's count the cash! I tortured the hell outta both of 'em till I made them talk!"

"*Who?*" Sandy blurted. Stunned and perplexed, she wondered, *Did he rob the wrong couple? Was there actual money in the shopping bag?*

That last question was answered when he dumped out the contents onto the kitchen table.

Packs of currency wrapped with rubber bands tumbled out in a heap.

"See?" he said to Sandy. "You were right, by god! The old geezers weren't reporting their cash sales to the IRS! They were salting it away right in their house—they couldn't give themselves away by depositing it in a bank. They had money stashed everywhere—and I didn't stop working on 'em with lit cigarettes till I was sure they blabbed all the locations. Before I shot-gunned 'em, I made sure they had told me the truth. I pulled lumps of currency from under the carpets, under the linoleum, inside the TV and behind picture frames, places like that."

"You did a good job," Sandy allowed, still flab-bergasted.

"C'mon, let's add it up!" Bradley enthused, and he sat down in front of the pile of wrapped-up currency.

Sandy sat on a chair to one side of him, and they started undoing the rubber bands, some of which were so old, discolored, and brittle that they broke. As they counted each packet, they marked its total on a Post-it note. Sandy didn't believe that Bradley would have come directly here with all the money without hiding a good chunk somewhere for himself alone, because she would've done that very same thing. Still, what he had dropped on the table and was owning up to came to fifty-seven thousand dollars. A nice haul. And a motive to kill.

She hadn't expected the wild goose chase she had sent him on to actually be productive in the way of cash. But now he had succeeded beyond his wildest dreams—and hers. The trouble was, there were two brand-new murders that they both could be arrested for, he as perpetrator and she as mastermind—a label she had earned inadvertently, but it would make no difference to the cops because in the eyes of the law, she was as guilty as he was.

Even worse, for the past week, his photo had been all over the news again, the detectives working the previous murders and kidnapping obviously stumped and seeking help from the media. Sandy had to worry about what if somebody had spotted her and Bradley with Allison in Kennywood Park? And what if the photo on TV prompted them to come forward?

It seemed like Bradley Kelter was becoming more and more of a liability.

Still fired up over his newly acquired wealth, he said, "I've gotta tell Allison about this!"

"What do you mean, what she thinks?" Sandy said. "She's not even going to be around very long. In fact…I have something to tell you. I'm sorry, Bradley, but when I went into her room this afternoon, I found her dead."

Bradley immediately burst into huge, racking sobs and flung his head down onto the kitchen table, right on top of a stack of money.

Sandy let him cry for a long while. Then she said, "She had wriggled out of the rope around her left wrist, and she stuffed a Tampon down her throat from the box of them on the nightstand. I pulled it out, but it was too late. She died of suffocation. I never thought she'd commit suicide. We should've been more watchful."

"What did you do with her?" Bradley managed to squeak out between sobs.

"Well...you know..." Sandy replied.

He got the picture and sobbed even louder.

27

Three days after the robbery and double murder of the husband and wife who grew pine trees—an occurrence that so far Detective Delaney and Spivak knew nothing about—they were riding on a country road in their unmarked sedan. They had already spoken with dismay about the fact that the first murder on their plate —Jackie Kelter's—had taken place back in June, and here it was almost October, and the string hadn't been solved.

From behind the wheel, Vince said, "I didn't really expect a fast result, or any result to be honest."

He was referring to Sheriff Patton's consent to let them put Bradley Kelter's photo on TV.

Jerry said, "Every now and then, a blind pig gets an acorn."

Vince almost wanted to laugh but didn't. He said, "Not funny, Jerry. If the guy that owns the feed store wasn't bullshitting us, the hogs are getting more than acorns. How much farther?"

"That looks like it, up there, that low building with

the loading dock. I'm anxious to take the guy's statement, see if he's just making it up."

Vince negotiated the next two hundred yards or so on the potholed two-lane blacktop, then pulled the car off the road and parked in front of the feed store to the left of the loading dock. He and Jerry got out and looked all around, seeing no one, and went up concrete steps into the store.

A doorbell rang, and a big redheaded potbellied guy in rumpled brown trousers, bibbed coveralls, and a wife-beater shirt came out from behind rows of steel shelves and said in a gruff voice, "You guys must be the cops."

"Homicide detectives, sir," Jerry replied. "Are you Judd Sheppard?"

"Used to be and still am. I don't like what I suspect is goin' on around here."

Vince said, "We're here to investigate, Mr. Sheppard. Provided we have cause to."

"Call me Judd. You coulda knocked me over with a feather, but I swear he looks like that picture on the TV."

Vince said, "Who does, Judd?"

Jerry took a copy of the photo in question out of his inside suit-coat pocket. "Is this the picture you saw?"

"That's it all right, the same one. The lady on the news called him Bradley Kelter and said he was wanted for murdering his wife. Well, I swear he's been workin' as a handyman or somethin' for a customer of mine—a farm lady, name of Sandy Jacobs. I told one of you guys as much on the phone. Nobody knows much about her. She keeps a bunch of hogs that stink to high heaven, so nobody goes there very much. And they're scared to 'cause the place seems so spooky."

"Spooky in what way?" Jerry asked.

Judd Sheppard's voice got louder and angrier. "I don't

know what she feeds to those hogs of hers, but she don't seem to buy enough *feed* offa me. There's some sick rumors goin' around, but I don't wanna repeat what I heard 'cause I don't wanna get sued and lose my livelihood."

He pulled a can of snuff out of his bib pocket, pinched some off and put it in his mouth.

Jerry asked him, "Can you give us directions to Miss Jacobs's farm?"

"Sure can. But don't ask me to lead you there, fellers."

Vince and Jerry jumped back into their car, and Vince said, "I guess I would've liked to question Judd Sheppard some more."

"Yeah," Jerry agreed. "We'll need to bring him in for a formal statement. But I didn't want to do it right now. Because while we'd be doing it, Kelter could fly the coop, and we'd never get another lead on him." All of a sudden he said, "There's the turn-off, Vince!"

Vince squealed the tires in an abrupt left turn onto a dirt road, then they kept going, slowing down and bouncing over ruts, till they were almost to the foot of the farm's driveway, where Vince pulled over and stopped, barely leaving room for any other vehicle to get by, and Jerry automatically knew that he didn't want to get close enough to the farmhouse to spook

Bradley Kelter if he was on the premises and keeping an eye out.

Warily, they got out of the unmarked and looked all around.

Vince said, "This whole place looks deserted. I don't see the Jeep Kelter is supposed to own or any other vehicle, for that matter."

Jerry said, "Let's have a look down there by the barn.

Maybe she's feeding the animals. I can smell them from here."

"Yeah, I could smell them from the moon," Vince replied

They crept slowly down to the hog pen, the stench getting worse and worse as they approached. They didn't go right up to it because of the smell.

"*Peeyew!*" Vince exclaimed, wrinkling his nose. "This is close enough! I can't stand the stink! Can you?"

"Hell, *no!*" Jerry barked. "Shoulda brought my Vicks."

The hogs were shoving and butting against one another, greedily gorging on something, but they couldn't make out what it was.

Vince said, "Maybe this Sandy person is in the barn. Let's have a look before we go up to the house."

"You just want to get away from the hog stink," Vince quipped.

"I think we'll still smell it," Jerry said. "We'll even smell it in the car and when we get home. it'll be in our clothes."

Like the smell of death when we've been on a murder scene, Vince thought, but he didn't say so out loud.

They both entered the barn, keeping their hands on their holstered weapons, just in case someone was lurking in there, ready to jump them. But the barn was empty of either humans or livestock. There were no horses in the stalls, no cows mooing, no chickens clucking around. So without a word, they turned around and headed back toward the house.

They went up onto the porch, pounded on the door, and were momentarily startled when

Sandy opened it and stood there smiling at them.

"Good afternoon, gentlemen," she said brightly. "What can I do for you? You don't look like salesmen or

Jehovah's Witnesses, although they're pretty much the same thing, just different wares." She laughed lightly at her own observation.

Jerry said, "You're the owner, Miss Sandy Jacobs?"

"Yes, I am. Have I done something wrong?"

She was wearing a yellow sweater and black jeans, which showed that she had a nice trim figure. Jerry guessed from her slightly slackening face that she was probably in her midforties but in great shape for her age. She had a mildly mocking sort of smile, half mischievous and half sly, Jerry thought, and undeniably sensual—the kind of woman who could wrap a man around her little finger even as she was wearing him out in bed. He didn't usually entertain those kinds of thoughts about women, but this time he found himself doing so. She seemed alluring but in a strange way that he couldn't put his finger on.

Meantime, Vince was saying, "It's not that we think you've done anything wrong, but you apparently have a handyman who's working for you, and he may be a different story."

"Oh, my! But he's gone. I fired him. It's been over a week ago now, and I have no idea where he went. I don't *want* to know either. He was stealing from me, and even before I caught him at it, I thought he was sneaky and weird."

"Do you know his name?" Vince asked. "I mean, whatever name he gave you?"

"He said it was Bradley Jefferson. I paid him in cash. I admit I never filed paperwork on him. I was going to, but he wasn't here long."

Jerry said, "We're not interested in that, Miss Jacobs. We're investigating a homicide. This is his picture. Take a close look at it."

He handed her a photo of Bradley Kelter, and she looked at it and gasped. "Oh my god! That's him, all right! I knew there was something weird about him! I guess I'm lucky he's not around anymore!"

"He's definitely a person of interest," Jerry advised her. "Are you sure you don't know where he lives now?"

Sandy shook her head sadly and said, "I wish I could tell you more, but like I said, he was sneaky and secretive, and I found that I couldn't trust him."

"When he showed up here, what was he driving?" Vince asked.

"Some kind of Jeep, yellow and black."

"That's definitely our guy," Vince said to Jerry. "We already have the license plate, so let's update the BOLO on his Jeep with a high alert for lawmen in this part of the state."

Jerry said, "I don't see any vehicles around here, Sandy. How do you manage without one?"

"I can't, for long, but my pickup truck is getting new tires put on it to hopefully pass inspection. I'll have it back maybe as soon as tomorrow."

"Well, be really careful if Bradley Jefferson ever shows his face here again for any reason," Jerry warned her. "We think his real name is Bradley Kelter, and he's probably armed and dangerous. Protect yourself—and tip us off right away. I'm going to give you my card."

"Well I already feel safer for having talked with you," Sandy said with a sigh and an ingratiating smile.

"Stay in touch," Vince told her, "especially if you have any kind of encounter with your ex-handyman, even a brief phone call. Let us know. If you can get him to tell him where he's residing, so much the better. Let's hope he didn't leave the state because that would probably mean a long manhunt. And we might never track him down."

Sandy took the card from Delaney, and then with a worried look on her face, she watched the detectives get in their car and leave.

About fifteen minutes later, Bradley pulled up in her pickup truck, got out, and headed toward the porch.

Just then, Sandy barged out with her shotgun.

Bradley jumped back, startled to see her pointing the gun directly at *him*.

"What the hell?!" he blurted. Then he panicked and started to run.

She fired one of the barrels—but missed.

By this time, he was running around the back end of the barn, and she was coming after him hot and heavy.

He ran into the woods behind the barn and hid behind a huge boulder.

She slowed down and prowled slowly after him, her eyes searching everywhere.

He drew his knife from the sheathe on his belt, then climbed on top of the boulder as quietly as he could, hoping that it was tall enough that she might not see him if she didn't look up. He waited for her to approach, and when she stopped by the boulder, seemingly unaware of his presence, he tried to jump down on her heavily and feet first so he could knock her down and stab her to death—but she jumped back so fast that he failed to get a good hold on her and he ended up crashing to the ground so hard that he dropped his knife. He scrambled for it—but she whirled on him with her shotgun, pulled the trigger, and sent a spew of heavy pellets crashing into his chest, shredding his upper torso.

Breathing hard, she stood over his gory body for a

long while. Then she found herself speaking to him, as she had to Allison as if he were still alive.

In many ways, it was a weird kind of eulogy. Standing over his gory body, she said, "In many ways, we were kindred spirits, but I'm sorry, honey, you had to go. I'm not willing to take any chances, and the cops have tracked you down, and they're too close for comfort. I tried to teach you all I know, but you really aren't all that bright, and it finally caught up with you. And it will mean a lot to my hogs if they're not too stuffed already. But if they are, I'll take what's left of you and Allison to that burn pit where we—"

She stopped herself in mid-sentence as a bright idea came to her.

"Hold on a minute, Bradley. That cop said to phone him right away if you came back here—and you did! He gave me his card, I have it in my pocket."

She bent over Bradley's bloody body, picked up his knife, and laid it next to him on the ground. Then she pulled Detective Delaney's card from her pocket, along with her cell phone, and punched in his number. She knew that he and his partner probably weren't far away in the short time they had left her, so she wasn't surprised when he answered right away on his cell phone.

Acting badly shaken and breathing in short gasps, she blurted, "That bastard Bradley just came back here—to kill me. He came at me with his knife, but I was ready with my shotgun, and I shot him. He's dead."

"Stay there," Jerry said with tense excitement. "We're only a few miles away. We'll make a quick U-turn."

Sandy said, "You won't have to worry about *him* anymore. He's a bloody mess, and I'm all shaken up over it. I'm going in the house for a sedative to settle me down."

"What did you shoot him with?" Jerry managed to get in.

"My shotgun. I had to have some kind of weapon living out here. Thank god I never had to use it till now. I'm going to hang up now. Please get here fast."

She ended the call and went into the house, leaving the shotgun lying on the ground next to Bradley's body.

The two detectives returned shortly, and when Sandy heard them approaching on the dirt driveway, she went back out. Jerry and Vince parked and got out of their car in a huge hurry—and saw Sandy standing over Bradley's dead body, appearing shocked and scared. They went over to her and grimly took in the whole scene, and they both realized that they shouldn't readily buy in to her explanation.

Vince said, "Look, Sandy, this looks like a legitimate self-defense situation, but there has to be a formal ruling. That means you'll need to be interviewed, give a signed statement, and so on. There will be an autopsy and a coroner's report."

Maintaining her pose of innocence, Sandy said, "I don't know how I can ever repay you for coming here and giving me a warning. If you hadn't done that, I would not have kept my shotgun within reach."

"Don't be too quick to thank us till you're cleared," Jerry advised her. "Till then, bear in mind that we may become your worst enemies, particularly if there's an inquest and charges are brought against you."

"Oh, I don't think that will happen," Sandy said. "After all, I've done nothing wrong."

In spite of her protestations, when Sheriff Patton and his uniformed deputies arrived, they took her into custody. She was taken away in a patrol car and was going to be held in the county jail till she could be interrogated and a district attorney could make a determination as to what would be done with her next.

The sheriff debriefed Jerry and Vince, and then they were allowed to head out. In their unmarked car, Jerry phoned his wife Jenny to give her a short version of what had transpired and also to ask her to put the kids on the line for a short burst so he could hear their voices and their laughs.

Vince then phoned Melissa and asked her to wait up for him. He was mostly tightlipped, not wanting to traumatize her over the phone, but he knew he was going to have to deliver news about her brother that might hit her hard even if she might not be aware of potentially blocked-out feelings about him.

Vince looked at his cell phone screen as he ended the call with Melissa and saw that it wasn't too late for him to stop and buy a bottle of wine. Maybe it might help ease the pain, if there should be any.

At the sheriff's office, he jumped out of the unmarked police car and let Jerry take the wheel. Then he got into his own vehicle, a Chevy Blazer. He bought wine at a grocery store, then drove straight to Melissa's apartment, where he tried to break it to her as gently as he could that her brother had been shot and killed. Somewhat to his surprise, she took it very hard and burst into hurtful sobs.

During a moment when her tears stopped flowing, she said, "I guess a part of me still loves him, not the real him, but my image of him as the brother he ought to have been."

"Maybe you always had a vague hope that he'd change," Vince said. "A miracle would happen, he'd have some sort of catharsis, and things between the two of you would be made right. A great healing would take place, and he'd become the brother you always dreamed of."

Melissa looked straight into Vince's eyes for a long moment, then she threw herself into his arms and held him tight. They stayed that way for a long time. Then she kissed him more passionately than she had ever done before.

Their lovemaking was intense. So much so that it didn't end with the first time. And it *felt* like the first time, too.

Afterward, they snuggled, and he opened the bottle of wine. It was like a sacrament, a toast, a promise of a new beginning for both of them.

He wasn't sure it would last. Maybe it wouldn't. But he was hopeful, and he sensed that she was too. He sensed that this breakthrough would not have happened except for the fact that she was now free of her brother like she had never been before, and as a result, she was able to start emerging from her blanket of fear.

28

Sheriff Patton decided that he would take charge of the interview with Sandy Jacobs while Detectives Spivak and Delaney went to work digging up background information on her. And at the same time, two more detectives headed to her farm with a CSI team to do an on-the-scene examination of Bradley Kelter's shot-gunned body and determine if there was any accompanying evidence that might tend to prove or disprove Sandy's story about how he met his demise.

In an interrogation room at county police headquarters that was wired for audio and video, the sheriff began by stating, "Subject Sandy Jacobs has consented to this interview of her own free will, and has been read her rights and has signed off on them. She has been advised that she is being recorded and videotaped for the record and that anything she says may be used against her in a court of law. Now, Miss Jacobs, are you ready?"

"Yes, Sheriff. I'm going to maintain my claim of self-defense."

"Well, you'll definitely be entitled to do that if and when you are charged, arraigned and prosecuted. Till then, you are presumed to be innocent until we have good reason to believe that you are guilty of a crime. I must warn you, however, that a search warrant has been issued, and investigators are on your property at this very moment. Therefore, it behooves you to tell us about any wrongdoing you are aware of, on the part of Bradley Kelter, yourself, or anyone else before we discover it for ourselves."

Sandy said, "I'm not worried because I haven't done anything wrong."

"If that's the case, would you be willing to take a polygraph?"

"Not today. Let's see if we can use this interview to convince you of my innocence."

"All right, then. First question. At any point during your acquaintanceship with Bradley Kelter, did he tell you that he had murdered his wife, Jackie?"

"No, I would've been scared of him, but I wouldn't have let him know that, and I would have turned him in the first chance I got."

Sheriff Patton eyed her sternly and asked, "Is there any chance that Jackie Kelter is buried on your property?"

"Not that I know of," she answered, unruffled and taking it in stride. "But now that I'm wise to so much more about Bradley, I wouldn't put it past him. Maybe he had her body in his Jeep, for all I know, just waiting for me to shop for groceries or something so he could have the run of the place."

"Speaking of his Jeep, do you have any idea where it might be?"

"Not really, but one would think that if he actually

used to transport the body of his murder victim, he might have taken it someplace and torched it."

The sheriff refrained from commenting on that answer but thought it was pretty damn perspicacious of her. In other words, she knew how to think like a criminal. That didn't prove she was one, but it might be an indication.

To try to shake her up, he said, "Have you ever noticed any areas in your fields or the adjoining property that might appear to be freshly dug up?"

She appeared to take it in and mull it over. Then her answer came, and it was slow and measured. "Well, Sheriff, since I don't really plant fields full of crops, not even crops used to feed my hogs, it's not like I spend a lot of time out in my fields. I pay a guy who has a tractor to keep the weeds down by coming here to mow them every couple of weeks as needed. Believe me, it's a load off my mind to have it taken care of."

"How *do* you feed your hogs?" Sheriff Patton asked pointedly. "Because we've heard some bizarre rumors." He already knew what had been said to Detectives Delaney and Spivak by the man who owned the feed store, and that was what had prompted him to suddenly take this tack.

"I buy a certain amount of what I give them to eat," Sandy said. "And I give them slops from the kitchen, husks and rinds and potato peels and such that I keep in a big garbage pail so I can go out and yell *soowee* and make them come running."

"I've seen Detective Delaney's photos from his cell phone," said the sheriff. "Those beasts look especially well-fed."

"Please don't call them beasts," Sandy chided. "They're more intelligent than almost every other creature, and they have some qualities that are almost human-like. You can realize that if you just think about why they are made to contribute heart valves to humans whose hearts are failing."

"Pardon me," said the sheriff. "But to hear you talk about them, it seems you might value those hogs more than you value people."

"They do less harm than people," said Sandy. "Especially when it comes to folks as evil as Bradley Kelter."

"Well, you certainly made sure he can't do any more evil," the sheriff said with dismay.

He couldn't shake the feeling that there were parts of her story that left important things out, but he couldn't prove it yet.

He didn't know that the proof would soon be forthcoming from the investigative teams working forty miles away at Sandy's farm. And when the news broke, the entire nation was stunned by what they saw and heard on TV. A breaking news report by anchorwoman Stacie Graver, reading her TelePrompTer with breathless excitement on a network affiliate in Pittsburgh, was typical of the coverage that incited the shockwaves.

"There has been an astounding development in the case of Miss Sandy Jacobs, a trans woman currently in police custody. It has been revealed that earlier in her bizarre life when she was a male who yearned to be a female, she actually spent twenty years in the United States Marine Corps and was awarded a Bronze Star and a Purple Heart for combat in Afghanistan…"

The TV showed cut-away shots of Sandy as a young man in uniform, first in dress blues and then in camouflage fatigues, as Stacie Graver continued her report:

"Sheriff's deputies have found human remains in a hog pen on Miss Jacobs's farm, and it appears that these remains must be those of a young woman named Allison Cisneros, whose boyfriend, James Cardoza, was found murdered on the same day that Allison disappeared from their school picnic at Kennywood Park. The investigators also discovered a burn pit that may have been used to dispose of the body of Jackie Kelter, the estranged wife of Bradley Kelter, a fugitive who was shot to death by Miss Jacobs while police were trying to track him down to question and perhaps charge him with his wife's murder."

There was video footage of the rooting hogs, the burn pit, and various body-sized holes that the police had dug up in various parts of Sandy Jacobs's property as Stacie Graves wrapped up her report:

"The CSI team dug at least fifty holes all around Ms. Jacobs's farm, and no additional human remains were found, but local residents told police that people had been disappearing mysteriously for several years while they were under her employ. This bizarre criminal investigation continues, and you can keep up with it right here on Action News."

Sheriff Patton and Detectives Delaney and Spivak, all of them bone-tired from the day's demands and tribulations, watched the late-breaking news report in the sheriff's conference room and lamented that they were a long way from gathering enough evidence and witness statements, if any, to bring Sandy Jacobs to trial, much less convict her, because she had effectively raised the prospect of so-called "reasonable doubt" by killing Bradley Kelter. All it would take would be one stubborn jury member who would be suckered into believing that Kelter was the murderer and had committed all the crimes behind Sandy's back.

Nevertheless, Vince Spivak pressed Sheriff Patton on

going forward by saying, "We've got to at least charge her, put a lot of pressure on her to see if she folds. There's a good chance she'll confess if we offer a plea."

"That'd be up to the prosecuting attorney—if we ever get that far," the sheriff said. "As it stands right now, we don't have enough to even begin to pitch our case. I don't think we have it nailed down enough. Not if she gets an excellent defense attorney, and apparently she has a lot of money and we think we know how she got it but we can't prove it."

"From robbing and murdering that coin dealer," Jerry interjected.

"We think that, except we have no evidence," said the sheriff. "No fingerprints, no telltale bloodstains, and no witnesses willing to come forward. A top-notch defense attorney, or even one who's not so top-notch, will be shrewd enough to put it all on Bradley Kelter, and it'll be tough to prove otherwise. She might even take the stand, and she's totally believable when she wants to be. They'll claim that Kelter did all the dirty work on his own, and so she did the world a favor when she killed him—and furthermore, she had to, because she was in fear for her life."

They stopped talking because a follow up report by Stacie Graver came on the air and they wanted to watch it. It was a good way for them to gauge what was being fed to potential jurors out in the community.

"Sandy Jacobs, now known as the 'Hog Woman,' has been jailed, and her animals have been euthanized. The LGBTQIA+ community is outraged. Their spokesperson said that Miss Jacobs can never get a fair trial because of sexual and lifestyle prejudices, even though she is not guilty of any crime and, to the contrary, has acted purely in self-defense.

"Interviews with LGBTQIA+ representations followed, intermixed with general man-in-the-street opinions. Some people stated that Sandy Jacobs was innocent until proven guilty and should be treated that way, the same as anybody else would be. Others said she was a demented freak who should be immediately given the death penalty."

Sheriff Patton was holding the remote, and he shut the TV off.

"See what I mean?" he said. "How the hell would a prosecutor ever wade his way through that kind of shit and come up with an impartial jury?"

"I don't know," Jerry answered. "We've got our work cut out for us. We need some kind of break because I don't believe she'll ever confess."

———

BUT THE NEXT DAY, to their great surprise, Sandy Jacobs decided to take a plea.

Sheriff Patton was in the conference room early in the morning on a Wednesday, waiting for Detectives Delany and Spivak to show up. He was fidgety from already knowing something that they didn't, and he paced around looking over and over again at evidence photos taped to a whiteboard showing the incriminating sites on Sandy's farm, and he looked up when Jerry and Vince entered with cups of coffee in their hands. A big box of doughnuts was already on the table and they each grabbed a doughnut and a napkin, and the sheriff piped up.

"Guess what, guys—are you ready for this? She's decided to confess and plead guilty by reason of insanity.

She even fired her lawyer, one of the top legal beagles in the country."

"Huh?!" Vince blurted. "This is a joke, right?"

Jerry said, "What the fuck? Are we living in a twilight zone?"

"No joke, gentlemen," Sheriff Patton said. "She's afraid she'll get convicted now that we have another key witness."

"That's news to us," Jerry said, startled. "Who came forward?"

"One of my deputies tracked down the crooked pawn-shop guy who fenced the coin collection stolen from Mr. and Mrs. Warner. He folded and took a plea deal. He said that Sandy Jacobs, not Bradley Kelter, brought the coin collection to him, and it wasn't the first time he'd bought stolen goods from her. He said he was aware that all the things he fenced came from people she killed."

"And fed her to hogs!" Vince blurted incredulously.

The sheriff said, "Right. And I wish we could prove it. We're gonna try. But maybe she'll confess to all of it as part of her insanity defense."

"Sounds like she's wacky enough," Jerry said. "Who's going to interrogate her?"

"I'll take a whack at it," Sheriff Patton said. "I want you two to be there."

Less than an hour later, they had Sandy sitting across from them in a chair that was bolted down. Although she was in chains and handcuffs and wearing a rumpled orange jumpsuit that was baggy on her, she truly looked like what she had made herself into; a haughty and maturely attractive woman who was smart and worldly wise, and able to dominate most men.

The sheriff began by saying, "You don't want a lawyer present?"

Bemusedly, Sandy said, "Come on, you already know I fired the one I had. And don't want another one. They don't want me to do this. They just want the notoriety of representing me through a long, drawn-out trial."

"Is it true that you're ready to confess?"

"I'm going to tell you everything, Sheriff. Including things that you don't even know about yet."

And so, on the six o'clock news that day, anchor-woman Stacie Graver said, "The gruesome details of this case keep getting more and more strange and night-marish as they unfold. Sandy Jacobs, now known as the Hog Woman, has freely and openly confessed to seventeen additional murders, but police teams with shovels, picks, and backhoes have dug holes all over her property —and found nothing to corroborate her gruesome stories! So, is she lying? Or is she telling the god-awful truth? Earlier today, after a thorough interrogation, Sheriff Patton said that she is definitely one of the most devious killers he has ever faced and that, in his opinion, she wants to get herself committed to an asylum instead of a maximum-security prison, where she might eventually get released or else be able to escape."

Over the next five weeks, leading into Thanksgiving weekend, Vince Spivak and Jerry Delaney followed the tangled manipulations and strategies of the Allegheny County court system as it tried to come to a determination as to Sandy Jacobs's sanity or insanity. Meantime, she languished in a jail cell in the huge, outwardly modern, monolithic county jail on Second Avenue in downtown Pittsburgh because her bail had been set by Judge Rotelli, a fervent "family values" Republican, at five million dollars, an amount that she apparently did not have enough stolen money to pay.

Protest marches by pro-LGBTQIA+ folks as well as

anti-gay and anti-LGBTQIA+ folks had never let up ever since Sandy was first arrested, and Judge Rotelli tried to gain some sort of reprieve from their complaints and slanders by ruling that Sandy could be provided the drugs that helped maintain her femininity throughout her incarceration. The region's leading newspaper, which had a decidedly Republican bias, ran one editorial board article after another decrying the fact that taxpayers were now footing the bill for a procedure that was, in the vociferous words of strident Christian clergy, "unnatural and ungodly."

———

VINCE SPIVAK and Melissa Kelter joined the Delaney family for a Thanksgiving feast at their house, where the happy couple announced that they were getting married come December, and she was pregnant. As Jerry had predicted, Jenny was thrilled when Melissa asked her to be her maid of honor.

It was an Indian summer kind of day, weather-wise, brightly sunny and not too chilly for Vince and Jerry to go outside after everybody gorged themselves and had cigars and brandy by the pool, which had already been covered for the winter. They were not regular smokers, but once in a while, on special occasions like this one, they indulged in cigars that they never enjoyed as much as they thought they might.

"Too harsh on my throat, as usual," Jerry said. "Let's put 'em out and make do with more brandy."

As he poured the liquor, Billy and Janie came out to see what was happening, and he told them to go back in and put their jackets on.

While they were still alone without the kids around,

Vince said to Jerry, "Have you been following all the shit that's been going down?"

"Of course. It makes my blood boil," Jerry said, knowing that Vince was referring to the Sandy Jacobs's fiasco.

"I think she's angling for a short stay in a mental ward, after which she can get declared cured," Vince said.

"Me, too," Jerry agreed. "Then some do-gooder liberal psychiatrist might turn her loose on society."

"God forbid," Vince muttered.

"Stranger things have happened," Jerry said. "Strange and ridiculous. Like the sex offenders who get paroled for good behavior, then go out and take up where they left off. Like that creep in Florida who kept that poor little five-year-old girl locked in his closet for two weeks, then buried her alive while she was hugging her teddy bear."

"Just thinking about it makes me want to cry," Vince said. "The bastards should all be shot. Everybody knows they can't ever be rehabilitated, but the system pretends otherwise."

"The thing I dread," said Jerry, "is not so much that some asshole might diagnose Sandy as totally cured, but that she might be able to escape from wherever she gets put away. A mental ward is easier to escape from than a prison cell. I think that's what she's angling for."

Vince said, "Let's hope the psychiatric evaluation goes against her. I wish they had to ask *my* opinion before they could make their ruling."

"I'd leave her in jail till she rots," Jerry said adamantly.

"If she gets out, I'm afraid Melissa might backslide," Vince told him. "Things between us are going so much better now that I don't want any sudden downturn that could set her back."

"Let's hope that Republican judge does the right thing," said Jerry. "I want to see Sandy put on trial, convicted, and doing hard time."

"Hard time is right unless she's kept in her cell, away from the other horny prisoners."

"Can you imagine the circus that will be?" Vince said. "Who's gonna decide if she belongs in a male or female prison? I guess female."

"Yeah, that sort of makes sense," Jerry agreed.

They clammed up suddenly, because the two kids came back outside not only with their jackets on but also with softball gloves and a ball.

Janie said, "Play catch with us, Daddy!"

"You and Vince!" Billy chimed in. "We have extra gloves."

They tossed the extra gloves toward Vince and Jerry, who tried but failed to catch them in mid-air. They pulled the gloves on, and the kids delightedly said, "Yay!" and "Right on!"

Vince and Jerry tried to put Sandy Jacobs out of their minds and be all smiles for the kiddies.

29

S andy Jacobs believed she had been through so much counseling, head shrinking and brain meddling that she could do a top-notch snow job on any psychiatric professional or board of professionals that came at her. To arm herself for the battle, she learned everything she could about the process and the potential outcomes by milking her lawyer before she fired him. He drove his points home with some amusing anecdotes sprinkled in. "The insanity defense has been around for about three centuries," he told Sandy. "In the 1300s, an English court freed a commoner who had shot and killed a Lord of Parliament because they decided he lacked the common sense to choose good above evil. And in the early 1800s in America, a guy who believed he was the rightful king of England tried to assassinate President Andrew Jackson so he could turn the country into a monarchy, and he was found delusional but extremely dangerous and kept in prison till he died."

Despite his predilection for entertaining himself with these sorts of pithy highlights, Sandy learned many things that were crucial to her, such as the differences between insanity and competency. Competency was evaluated while a person was arrested but not yet convicted, while insanity was evaluated at the time of the offense, in an effort to determine if he or she was legally insane while committing it. A ruling of insanity meant that, due to mental disease or defect, the defendant was incapable of either understanding the nature of the crime or distinguishing the difference between right and wrong. Being mentally incompetent to stand trial meant that the defendant was unable to understand the nature of the criminal proceeding or unable to assist counsel in the conduct of a defense.

Sandy was discouraged from going to trial by the fact that the insanity defense was only used in one percent of all cases, and in those select cases, it had racked up only a twenty-six percent success rate. She liked the statistic that it was used more successfully by women than men, but she had to wonder, in all practicality, if a jury with ingrained prejudices would consider male or female or something in between.

Defendants acquitted at trial were likely to spend as much time in a psychiatric institution as they would have if they had been tried and convicted. And if a defendant actually went on trial and was found to be not guilty by reason of insanity, the unlucky defendant would be sentenced to the maximum term allowed for the crime; then, after having served that maximum term and judged not to any longer a threat to the community, the original sentence could be extended every year for the rest of the offender's life.

All of these possible outcomes scared Sandy so badly that she desperately did not want to go before a jury. Her way out was that she had to secure a pretrial determination of "unfit to stand trial," which would have to be recommended by a forensic psychiatrist, who would report to a judge who had the power to declare her incompetent. He would rely heavily on the opinion of the evaluator as to Sandy's ability to understand the charges against her and the penalties she was facing and make wise decisions concerning her own welfare.

Sandy, who was inordinately proud of her intelligence and worldly wisdom, knew that she would have to reign it in in order to snow the judge. He had her totally under his thumb. Worst-case scenario was that he might order medication and treatment to make her competent enough to resume the court process and be put on trial. This outcome horrified her, and she needed to avoid it at all costs.

The last time she talked to the lawyer that she fired, he told her of one of his clients who pleaded guilty by reason of insanity and was still in a mental hospital after being put in there two decades ago. He was never sentenced to prison; he was ruled legally not responsible for the rape and murder he committed, but his insanity plea did not limit the duration of his confinement. The law that governed people who were acquitted because of mental illness dictated that they be hospitalized until they were deemed safe to be released, no matter how long that takes, and the end point for some reason had not ever been reached in the opinion of judge, jury and the mental institution. To Sandy, it sounded Kafkaesque. And it made her shudder.

As it turned out, her psychiatric evaluation happened quickly, within three weeks of her arrest. She was interviewed in her cell by Dr. Morris Feldman, a frail and sickly-looking elderly gentleman in a rumpled gray suit with a darker gray necktie, who wore bifocals in gold frames.

He turned on a small pocket-sized recorder and began by asking Sandy all about her childhood. This was all too perfect for her because she was able to hit him, in a shy and hurtful voice, about the abuse by her parents and their fanatical anti-gay preacher, his Council of Elders and his rabid congregation. She had a sense that Dr. Feldman might be gay, so she laid it on thick as she went into lurid detail about the savagely applied "conversion therapy" and "Rainbow Washing" that she had been ruthlessly subjected to, such as being held down by two big oafs while she was given improvised shock treatments with bare wires hooked to a car battery, plus being urged to imagine herself beating her father to bloody smithereens with a baseball bat, plus other embellishments that she skillfully added in even though they never happened. She made it all sound like the equivalent of being put on the rack and having her arms and legs torn out of their sockets or being burned at the stake during the Catholic Inquisition.

Through all of this recitation, she could tell that she had Dr. Feldman's rapt attention. She dared to think that she had him under her spell. Now she had to hope his report would slant her way, and that the right person would find it credible.

Once more, because of news leaks over the next two weeks, she was ripe fodder for public outcries and televised demonstrations on Second Avenue, the street in front of the jail, and she sometimes watched through the tall, narrow window of her cell which was reinforced by wire webbing. Sleeplessly she paced the cold, bare ten-by-ten floor, planning what her next move should be if Judge Rotelli ever ruled in her favor.

30

Sandy was handcuffed and in the back of an SUV, one cop driving and another one in the front passenger seat. Since she was not a jail prisoner but instead a patient-to-be in a sanatorium, she was not in an orange jumpsuit but in civilian clothes.

Sergeant Donovan said jeeringly, "You should be in prison for life or in the gas chamber, honey-pie. But thanks to our half-assed justice system, you got yourself into the nut house. Pretty damn cushy, if you ask me."

Not bothering to mask her insolence, Sandy said, "Then why don't you commit yourself if you think it's so groovy?"

The other cop, Corporal Fusco, said, "Watch your mouth. We could shoot you and say you tried to escape."

Sandy refrained from giving him a snotty reply, realizing that she had to start acting timid, like most men thought that a member of the weaker sex should be. She needed her two guards to buy into her act if she hoped to gain the upper hand.

She rode for a long time in watchful silence before

she finally told them, in a softly pleading voice, "I have to pee real bad. Will you pull over?"

Sergeant Donovan, the driver, leered at her in the rearview mirror and said, "I should let you piss yourself, but I'd kinda like to see how you do it since you don't got a dick anymore."

That did it. She couldn't help blurting, "I do it like a *woman*—you asshole!"

Both cops chortled uproariously. She was relieved that they didn't get mad at her and refuse to do anything she wanted.

She was gratified when Donovan pulled the SUV off the road a piece, then got out and unlocked the back passenger door and opened it to let her out.

He led her a short distance off the road, where she stopped and turned, purposely facing him and making eye contact.

"Keep movin'," he demanded. "We gotta deliver you on time."

Feigning extreme shyness, she said, "How am I supposed to pull my pants down if I'm in cuffs?"

Mulling it over, she finally said, "All right, I'll be a gentleman and unlock one of 'em, but remember I'm lookin' for a chance to shoot you, so don't try anything funny."

He got a key from a pouch on his belt and used it to unlock one of the cuffs, then led her into an area behind some shrubs—and she suddenly spun and judo-kicked him—right in his balls. In the same motion, she chopped him in the back of the neck—and she grabbed his gun out of its holster as he went down.

He was writhing and groaning on the ground in intense pain.

She told him, "I not only used to be a man, but I was

also a Marine. Don't judge a book by its cover. I was highly trained in hand-to-hand combat—you fucking jerk!"

She shot him in the head with his own pistol, then stooped over him and took a wad of money plus some credit cards out of his pocket. Then she looked up hastily to make sure that Corp. Fusco wasn't coming to see what the delay was.

He yelled from the direction of the SUV when apparently he decided that he had actually heard a gunshot.

"You killed her, Joe? Good! By doing it in the weeds, none of her blood got on the back seat."

Sandy heard him start laughing as she hurriedly picked up the handcuff key and undid the other handcuff.

Corp. Fusco almost choked on his laughter when he saw her coming toward him with Sergeant Donovan's gun.

She shot him twice in his head, right through the wound-down window. Then she dragged his body out of the vehicle, went through his pockets and took his money and credit cards, dragged him farther back in the weeds where he wouldn't be readily spotted, then got behind the wheel and drove off.

31

Sheriff Patton, Jerry Delaney, and Vince Spivak were in the sheriff's conference room watching a news report from Stacie Graver for which they had fed her the basic information.

"Chalk up two more vicious murders to the so-called Hog Woman. As she was being transported to the Woodville Sanatorium, Sandy Jacobs somehow got the drop on the two officers in charge of her and shot and killed them both. She is now a desperate fugitive with a string of murders under her belt, definitely armed and dangerous. If you should come in contact with her and recognize her from our news footage, do not approach her—immediately contact the County Sheriff's Department or this station, and phone 9-1-1. You can do it anonymously."

The sheriff and the detectives were flabbergasted and utterly dismayed over Sandy's escape and the murders of the two cops. Jerry said, "At least she made our announcement. Let's hope it stirs up some kind of a lead."

Sheriff Patton said gruffly, "I wish I never heard of Bradley Kelter and this fucking so-called Hog Woman! Now I've got two dead cops, and she's on the loose and armed with *their* weapons! How the hell could she have hoodwinked them?"

"She's just too damned clever," Vince said, "and she can make herself seem harmless. But she can't get far without money."

"She's got *their* money—and their credit cards, probably," Sheriff Patton said. "We don't know how much cash they might've been carrying."

Jerry said, "She's likely been killing people for years and living high on the hog—pardon the pun—off of her victims. She'll try to get started doing the same thing again someplace else—you can bet on it."

"We have a tracking order out on the officers' credit cards in case she's desperate enough to use them," the sheriff said. "We should be so lucky."

But Jerry said, "She could be anywhere by now. We should plaster photos of her on every TV station."

"Already done," said the sheriff. "She's been seen on the news every day anyhow, ever since this fiasco began. Let's hope somebody recognizes her and tips us before more people wind up dead."

32

S andy was sitting at the bar of a hotel cocktail lounge, smiling at a dapper young man whose reflection she had spotted in a panoramic mirror behind shelves of top-shelf liquors. He smiled back at her, also in the mirror, as if he liked what he was seeing from behind her and a few feet away. Without being invited except by the way they had been eyeing each other in the mirror, she got up from her stool, taking her glass of wine with her, and sat down opposite him in his booth.

"Well, hello, sweetheart," he said.

She said, "You're a handsome young fellow. I thought maybe you would like to take me to bed."

He said, "Are you a hooker? Or worse, a vice cop?"

"No, I won't take your money," she said saucily. "I'll only take you."

He grinned and chuckled. Then he ordered fresh drinks for both of them, and they started "getting to know each other" by telling lies. She knew she was lying and suspected that he was too, but told herself that some of what he was saying might even be true. Either way, she could not have cared less.

He had a full head of dark hair and was probably so young that it wasn't dyed. She pegged him at about thirty-five. He had nice dark eyebrows, a neat dark mustache, and a strong, square face with a cleft chin. He was wearing an expensive-looking blue sweater and black jeans, and the sweater had short sleeves that showed off his biceps, plus it clung to his pectorals in a way that showed her he was used to working out.

During their conversation, which they both knew was a form of foreplay, he revealed that he wasn't currently married but had been divorced twice. She smiled and said, "Same here." In a sly, assertive way, he said that he had never been to Pittsburgh and that normally he would have flirted with more than one woman before choosing one of them to take to bed, but that she had a sexy, uninhibited look that he really liked. And again, she said, "Same here," and they both laughed.

They never bothered telling each other their names, phony or otherwise. They both knew that this would be a one-time fling. *No* follow-up. No unwanted complications.

He sipped his martini and said, "Since you maintain that you're not a hooker, tell me what you do for a living. You look too flashy for some kind of a dull, ordinary career."

She said flippantly, "I lure men like you into my clutches, then I murder them and take all their money. I poisoned my two former husbands."

He got a good laugh out of that, then he said, "No. Really. What do you do?"

So she told him she was a sales rep for a pharmaceutical company and had been their top earner for the past three years. "I get a fat salary and huge bonuses, and they boosted me even higher when I made noises about getting offers from an even bigger company."

"That's great," he said admiringly, and his reaction seemed real. "I work for a major corporation also. We finance some of the big-budget Hollywood movies. *Black Panther* was one of ours, and also several other of the megahits from Marvel Comics."

"What're you doing here in Pittsburgh?"

"Making contact with the theater owners who are still playing major movies. They're unfortunately a dying breed. I think that pretty soon, in the near future, the indoor theaters will go the way of the drive-ins. Did you know that back in the fifties and sixties, there were twenty thousand drive-in movie theaters in this country? And now what are there? Maybe a hundred or maybe even fewer."

"No, I guess I didn't know that," Sandy said. "But then it's got nothing to do with the business I'm in."

"Which one?" he asked facetiously. "Selling drugs or killing husbands?"

She laughed, appreciating that he was just as flippant as she was while also relishing the way she was succeeding in manipulating him. He thought he was snowing her into believing he was a Hollywood hotshot, not realizing that she had been playing him from the jump.

After a while, he said, "You do realize that if I ask you whether or not you're a cop, which I have already done, and you answer no, which *you've* already done, then any sex solicitation charges pursuant to our encounter won't stick?"

"I do realize that, so let's finish our drinks."

They did so, then he left money on top of the bill,

which he weighted down with his moisture-beaded glass, and they both arose and she took him by his hand and led him toward the elevators.

She said, "We'll have to use your room. Mine is a mess, I'm afraid. I toss my things anywhere they happen to fall when I'm on these business trips."

"I keep my room neat for some reason," he said. "My mother trained me that way, and my wives appreciated it. Also, it's always ready for encounters like this one."

Sandy had observed the bartender with a suspicious look on his face as he had watched them go, and for a moment, she almost fled the scene for fear that he had recognized her from the images of her that had been on TV too many times for comfort—and it was titillatingly exciting to imagine that a pack of cops might burst in on them while they were stripped naked and she was on top of him, inflamed with passion, writhing and moaning and trying not to yell out loud.

As she climaxed, she pulled a knife from under her balled-up clothes and slit his throat.

He climaxed too and died with gouts of blood spurting from his severed aorta. She found that she enjoyed bathing in it and massaging it into her breasts and nipples, knowing that she would take a shower afterward and get dressed up and leave. She would also take his car keys if he had a car parked in the hotel garage, and abandon the one she had previously stolen, because it was getting too hot.

33

The young man's hotel room was the bloodiest that Delaney and Spivak had ever seen.

They wore long transparent plastic lab coats and plastic booties over their shoes, but there was still no way to get around the body without stepping in blood that squished and oozed. But even from the doorway, they had seen the wide gash in the victim's throat and his limp erection still oozing semen.

The mattress and the carpet around the bed were totally soaked, so much so that the pools of blood hadn't even started to coagulate even though the coroner's estimation, stated from a distance, was that he had been dead for about seven hours. That meant that he had likely been murdered around midnight.

Because he was naked, his wallet was in his trousers, which Delaney found in the little room with a TV, couch, and coffee table that adjoined the bedroom. The wallet contained a Pennsylvania driver's license with his name and address in Uniontown, which was about forty-two miles from Pittsburgh. His name was Thomas Caputo, and he was thirty-two years old. A business card in the wallet designated him as a computer programmer.

Jerry relayed all this information to Vince Spivak, who was still standing in the doorway to the murder room while the coroner had ventured further inside.

The coroner listened while Jerry filled Vince in, then said, "I can't do too much more right here. I'm going to have my men take him out on a gurney and transport his body bag to the morgue, where we'll clean it up and do the autopsy. I don't know if we'll learn much, but after we get him out of here, we'll look under the bed and under the other furniture in hopes of finding the murder weapon—but in all likelihood, the perp took it with him."

"It's a her, not a him," Vince said. "In fact, the bartender saw her leave with him to go up to his room, and his description of her fits Sandy Jacobs. How the hell he didn't call it in is beyond me."

Jerry said, "If he had ratted her out and he was wrong, it would have been bad for the hotel. Clientele would have dried up and they probably would've been sued."

"Well, his bad decision took a turn for the worse," Vince said.

34

Jerry and Vince were at County Police Headquarters till the wee hours filling out reports and talking things over with Sheriff Patton.

"Any idea why she does what she does?" the sheriff said, tugging on his goatee. "I read the psychiatrist's report that got Judge Rotelli to declare her incompetent, but I think it's a crock of shit. She's plenty competent when it comes to murdering people and getting away with it for all those years."

Jerry said, "I think one thing the psychiatrist said has some truth in it. His theory is that deep in her subconscious, she's killing, over and over again, the man she never wanted to be."

"But she kills women, too," Vince interjected.

Sheriff Patton said, "Self-hatred? Subconsciously killing herself? I don't like to wrestle with that kind of gobbledygook. There's a former FBI agent on one of those TV crime programs who always cuts through the bullshit and says they did it because they wanted to."

"Who cares why she does it?" Vince said with a

dismissive wave of his hands. "We just have to nail the bitch, and I don't know how we're going to do that."

Sheriff Patton said, "We have to catch a break. Somebody has to spot Sandy Jacobs and be sure enough that it's her to do the right thing and call it in. We've got a BOLO out on her, and it has to yield results before she kills again."

"Well, we know what she's probably driving," Jerry said. "The Volvo belonging to the fellow she killed. The hotel gave us the license plate number from when he booked his room."

Vince said, "I bet she's already got a stolen license plate on that Volvo. So the one that used to be on it is long gone."

"She's certainly smart enough to do that," Sheriff Patton agreed.

35

S andy Jacobs was proud of the way she had taken matters into her own hands during the past week and a half. After killing the two cops who were taking her to the psychiatric hospital, she needed to make her getaway in their SUV, but she knew she couldn't keep it for long, or she wouldn't have gotten very far. So she had hot-wired an innocuous white six-year-old Honda in a used-car lot that was shut down for the day. She had walked to it from a patch of woods a couple miles away, where she had ditched the SUV, figuring it probably wouldn't be discovered for a few days. Next she had stolen a license plate from a gray Kia parked in a suburban driveway and put it on the Honda so she could drive here and there for a while in relative safety.

Now she was behind the wheel of the Volvo that belonged to the fellow whose throat she had slit, and its current license plate was the same one that used to be on the gray Kia. She drove to a mall near the neighborhood where Jerry Delaney lived with his wife and two kids, which she had found out by doing some internet searches in a public library. She had watched Jenny Delaney drop the kids off at their school, then followed her to the mall. When she had entered the main entrance, Sandy was right behind her by a short distance, looking like any other innocent shopper. She was wearing an orange sweater and a short, thin, black leather jacket and also a black cloth hat pulled down low and designer sunglasses, so she wouldn't be easily recognized by those who might have seen her photo on the news. She had a large, sharp folding knife in her jacket pocket, the kind used by hunters to gut deer right where they were shot.

She had an itch to kill people who were cherished by the two detectives who had tried to put her either in the gas chamber or in prison for the rest of her life. She wanted to kill Jenny Delaney first, then Melissa Kelter, the sister that Bradley Kelter had hated. But she wasn't going to do it to avenge *him*. She didn't care about him. She didn't mind admitting to herself that she was crazy jealous of those two women simply because they had always been free to *enjoy* being women. They never had to go through life as biological mistakes.

Sandy was turned on by the prospect of leaving a bloody corpse somewhere in the mall where it would shock the hell out of *everybody*, including the cops. She recalled the creepy MO of the crazy nut known as the New Orleans Body Poser, who left his victims stark naked and lying on their backs with their legs spread. Under interrogation, he confessed that he didn't do it just to create gruesome erotic displays; he would actually return to the bodies for days afterward and have sex with them until they started to smell. There was apparently no limit to the ugly side of human sexuality, including necrophilia. Sandy told herself that at least she wasn't *that* sick! She just wanted to stick her middle finger up the noses of the smug, overly judgmental prudes who heaped derision and disrespect on people like her.

As she kept an eye on Jenny Delaney, at first she wondered why Jenny didn't go into the Wal-Mart or Macy's or any of the high-end boutiques where most women liked to shop. But then she got her answer because Jenny got on an escalator that took her to a lower floor where there was a food court—where Melissa Kelter was beckoning to her—and she headed straight to Melissa's table, obviously meeting up with her by prearrangement.

For a moment, this development left Sandy wondering what she should do. And to give herself time to think it out, she headed across the food court to a Starbucks, where she bought a latte and a blueberry muffin, then sat at a table about twenty feet from where Melissa and Jenny were seated. They both already had coffee and pastries before them that Melissa must have bought in anticipation of Jenny's arrival.

Sandy sipped her latte and watched them out of the corner of her eye, and the fact that she was doing so was masked by her sunglasses. She had a feeling that one or both of them would do some shopping after they had their coffees and pastries, because otherwise it made no sense for them to come to the garishly bright mall when they could've met up at a smaller and more intimate place. Sandy had to wait and see what they would do next, and in a little while, they got up and went toward the escalator, so she dumped the rest of her latte and got on the escalator some distance behind them.

Melissa peeled off and went into the Walmart, and Jenny meandered into the Toys "R" Us. Sandy had a choice to make. Which one should she stick with?

She chose Melissa. Partly because Melissa was the one with whom she had once tried to assist Bradley and partly because she could not easily envision killing someone in a place full of things for children.

Now the question for Sandy was: how to get to Melissa Kelter in a place where she could be murdered with impunity. As she followed Melissa into the Walmart, hopeful ideas swarmed through her head, such as, wouldn't it be lovely if her intended victim went into one of those closet-like booths for trying on clothes? Sandy envisioned herself tapping discreetly on the door to a booth and Melissa innocently unlocking it to see if she were being summoned by a clerk or another customer. Then Sandy could push her way in and slit Melissa's throat so swiftly and surely that she wouldn't be able to scream as Sandy closed the door on the falling body and the spurting arterial blood and walked very quickly out of the Walmart and to her stolen car.

But she recognized all that as pure fantasy on her part, and she considered herself to be a realist, a pragmatist, not a starry-eyed dreamer. Therefore she decided to simply embrace what seemed risky but eminently practical, which was to follow Melissa until she headed into an aisle that was relatively free of other customers who might interfere in a murder attempt.

It turned out that the unwitting would-be victim was not in the store to try on clothes. Instead, she headed for the hardware section, which Sandy thought might work out well for her because most of the early-morning shoppers were females, apparently not as interested as men would be in nuts, bolts, clamps, and cheap tools.

When Melissa headed into an aisle displaying steel shelving, Sandy pulled her knife and charged at her with the intent of stabbing her in her back, then slitting her throat as she went down. But it didn't work out that way because in accordance with her desire to become an FBI agent someday, Melissa had taken karate and Taekwondo lessons coupled with even more strenuous lessons in self-defense for women.

Sandy's knife cut into Melissa's shoulder as she spun away from the sound of softly advancing footsteps and delivered a judo kick that hit Sandy's solar plexus but not hard enough to do crippling damage.

Sandy jabbed her knife at Melissa's throat and opened a gaping wound on the right side. Then, like a beast compelled by the sight of blood, Sandy tried to slice Melissa's jugular, but the blade swished through thin air.

Melissa slipped in a pool of her own blood and went down hard, her arms, hands, and legs flailing. Sandy was looming over her, trying to deliver a direct stab to her torso, but even while she was flailing on her back, Melissa managed to kick Sandy hard in her throat.

Sandy started choking—and she turned and ran, hoping her larynx wasn't crushed.

Melissa struggled to her feet and tried to chase after Sandy but only managed a few halting steps before slipping and falling again.

By that time, a security guard, two Walmart clerks and three customers appeared in the hardware aisle.

One of the customers was already calling 911.

36

An EMS team arrived at the scene of the Walmart attack within minutes. They stopped the loss of blood from Melissa's wounds, started treating her for shock, and loaded her into an ambulance that sped to the nearest hospital.

Vince and Jerry got the bad news directly from Sheriff Patton, and they both headed immediately to where she had been taken. Jerry drove the unmarked sedan this time, figuring that Vince was too badly shaken to risk being behind the wheel.

Sheriff Patton was already at Jefferson Hospital ahead of them, and he met them in the lobby because Melissa was in the ICU. But a doctor had told him that she was stabilized and would probably be kept in the Intensive Care Unit overnight, just as a precaution, and would be transferred to a regular room the next afternoon.

"We're allowed to talk to her briefly, one at a time, though," the sheriff said. "I already did that. She knows for certain that her assailant was the one and only Sandy Jacobs, who is likely to be talking quite hoarsely now, because Melissa judo-kicked her in her throat, a hard blow that may have fractured her larynx. Witnesses said she turned and ran, coughing like mad and spitting up some blood."

"Too bad it didn't fracture her skull," Jerry said.

Vince said, "I can't wait to go up and see her. What floor is the ICU on?"

"Six," the sheriff said, and Vince promptly pivoted and headed straight to the elevators.

Jerry said, "Listen, Don, when you talked to Melissa, I realize it had to be brief, but did she say anything that could help us track Sandy down?"

"No, it wasn't possible for her to do anything but try to save her own life. And at least she pulled that off in fine style. If she were one of my deputies, I'd have to recommend her for a Certificate of Commendation."

"We can't leave her alone in this hospital," Jerry said. "There's a possibility that Sandy Jacobs might come after her if she's still able."

"I'll assign two guards to work shifts, spelling each other, and never take any breaks unless one of them stays nearby," the sheriff promised.

"How sure are we about Melissa's ID of the perpetrator.?"

"Oh, I'd bet my pension on it. But we'll get DNA from the blood and mucus she coughed up. That'll be the clincher."

"I wonder who she's going to go after next," Jerry said, hoping it wouldn't be anyone in his own family.

He knew that his wife had been meeting up with Melissa that morning, but they were going to shop in different stores after they had coffee. But for that simple, seemingly innocuous arrangement, he realized that Jenny might have been attacked along with Melissa, or at the very least, might have witnessed the attack, and that thought gave him the willies.

Like everyone else in law enforcement, he understood that matters of life and death often hinged on pure circumstance, which was another way of saying pure luck.

37

T wo weeks later, a few days short of the Christmas holidays, Melissa had recovered from her wounds, and things in the detectives' lives were almost back to normal, except Sandy Jacobs still had not been captured and her specter lurked over everything they did. They never felt completely safe, but they tried to pretend otherwise for the sake of their loved ones.

On a Friday when nothing too dramatic had happened during that week, Sheriff Patton said to them, "You both need some time to unwind. I'm afraid one of you will have a stroke or a heart attack. You're not too young for it to happen. Bad stuff happens when you push too hard. Go home to your loved ones for a change."

They protested half-heartedly, then finally gave in, thanked the sheriff, and headed for the exit. They were in the parking lot, about to get into their own cars, when Jerry said, "Do you and Melissa want to come to my house for dinner tomorrow evening? I'll be grilling steaks and Jenny will whip up a nice big salad to go with the baked potatoes done on the grill. I got a call from her while I was in the men's room. She was so glad when I told her I was coming home, she made me feel guilty for all the times I wasn't able to."

"Nah, you do the family thing, Jerry. Melissa and I need to do some more apartment hunting now that I've suddenly got a free evening. We'll grab some fast food at some point."

Jerry got into his car and drove away, and Vince backed his car out and headed in the opposite direction. Within a few minutes, he parked in from of a neighborhood bar with loud music escaping into the street. He went in, saw a group of three cops sitting at one of the tables, said his hellos, and sat by himself on a barstool.

One of the cops, a uniformed sergeant named Bill Cooley, got up and came over to him to ask, "How're things going on the Hog Lady thing?"

Jerry said, "If you've been watching the news, it's obvious we're bogged down."

"Shit! I hate to hear that," Sergeant Cooley said. "If it goes cold, the public will crucify us. Where's your sidekick?"

"He's gonna spend some needed time with his family while the case is goin' nowhere. I'm just in here for a couple quick drinks before I head to my fiancée's apartment. I don't like to leave her alone for long. I'm almost more worried about Jerry though. Remember the time that young killer came after him? He was damn lucky he survived. Good thing the killer didn't, if you ask me."

"I'm with you on that," said the sergeant. "Homicides are over the top these days because too few states have the death penalty. We ought to have the choice of taking them in dead or alive, like in the Wild West."

Not wanting to get into that kind of discussion, Vince said, "Jerry invited me to dinner with him and his wife and kids, and I took a rain check. But maybe I'll take a run over to his neighborhood just in case."

"I don't blame you. Us cops always gotta have our partners' backs. It don't work any other way, right?"

"Right on," Vince said.

38

J erry Delaney drove along his nice suburban street, admiring the peace and calm of it tonight and most nights in his recent memory. He pulled into his driveway, got out of his car and went up onto the front porch, and fished his key out of his pants pocket.

Bright headlights swept him, and he turned and looked but couldn't make out what kind of car it was. But it kept going, so he stared after it for a while, then unlocked the door and entered the house.

In the living room, Billy and Janie were sitting cross-legged in front of the TV, watching a cartoon show. Billy turned toward Jerry and got up slowly with his head still turned toward the cartoon, but Janie jumped up, wrinkling her face into a smile, and said, "Daddy!"

The kids came toward him, and he pretended to feint and jab at them like a boxer, and they put their dukes up the way he had taught them. They pretended to box for a while, then he hugged and kissed them while they were smiling and laughing.

Janie called out, "Mom! Daddy's home!"

Jenny came in from the kitchen wearing an apron, and she and Jerry hugged and kissed.

———

SANDY JACOBS PARKED the Volvo halfway down the block and at the dark edge of a pool of light from a streetlamp, then turned off the ignition, got out, and let the door go shut as softly as she could. She was wearing the same black clothing she had worn during her unsuccessful attack against Melissa Kelter. That was a week and a half ago, and the punishing effects of the kick to her neck had healed.

Moving swiftly and quietly toward the Delaneys' house, she cut through a neighbor's yard and into an alley to skirt around and behind a redwood fence, tested and found the gate unlocked, and let herself in. Then she crept across the lawn and pulled her knife out when she reached the side of the house. She considered cutting the wire that served the telephone landline and the one that provided electricity but rejected the notion, realizing that if the house suddenly went dark, it would alert the people inside that something was amiss.

———

IN THE LIVING ROOM, Jenny said to Jerry, "Oops! I don't want the steaks to burn. I put them on the grill as soon as you phoned and said you were on your way."

She hurried into the kitchen, opened the sliding glass door to the patio—and instantly got jumped by Sandy, who put her in a choke hold with the knife at her throat. She tried to yell for Jerry, but the choke hold turned her outcry into barely a splutter.

"Jerry—I-I-"

"Shut up, damn you!"

Jerry went for his gun—but froze. The two kids were absolutely shocked—and they jumped up from the couch as Sandy duck-walked Jenny in from the kitchen.

Sandy was smiling evilly, and Jenny was trying to talk but couldn't—until Sandy slightly relaxed her hold.

"Please don't hurt the children!" Jenny blurted chokingly.

Sandy scowled at Jerry, saying, "Drop that gun, Delaney, or I'll slit your wife's throat! And tell your two brats to sit down and shut their traps."

He stooped and laid his gun on the carpet, and she commanded, "Now back away from it!"

Jerry did what he was told, and Sandy shoved onto the floor as she grabbed the gun for herself. Now she was armed with a gun and a knife, and she chuckled with snide satisfaction at the whole situation, which was a triumph for her.

Jenny was still on the floor, crying, and Jerry took a chance and boldly helped her to her feet, then stepped in front of her as a shield.

Billy and Janie were still cowering on the couch.

When Sandy eyed Jerry malevolently, he forced himself to address her as calmly as he could, speaking in measured tones and throwing in some flattery as if he might be able to get her to delay her murderous intentions.

"I have to compliment you on the way you pulled this home invasion off, Sandy. How did you find out where I live?"

"Hmph! Don't try to stall me off by asking stupid questions. The internet was very helpful. Then I phoned your desk sergeant, pretending to be one of your favorite reporters—Stacie Graver. What an irony that pretty Miss Graver will soon realize she helped put you in your grave! And the asshole desk sergeant liked the way I talked to him, oh so sexy, like I could really go for a guy in a cop uniform, and I couldn't wait to get his dick in my mouth. Once he got the hots for me, even though I was just a voice over the phone, the stupid jerk told me everything I wanted to know."

Jerry desperately wanted to believe that where there was still life, there was hope, even though any notion that he and his family might be saved seemed so remote and futile that he couldn't even imagine how it could possibly come true. Going from a cajoling demeanor to a threatening one, he said, "You better get out of here while you still can. If you do us any severe harm, every cop in the state will be coming to hunt you down."

"Hah! They're doing that already, and look how much good it did *you*. Now sit down in that easy chair—because I'm going to make sure you go out *easy*. First, I'm going to shoot you in the head with your own gun. Then I'm going to kill your wife and kids—and make it look like it all happened in reverse. Poor you! Ending your career as a murder-suicide. I don't think you'll get a parade with bagpipes playing *Amazing Grace*—instead, you'll be considered a *disgrace!*"

"Bullcrap! Nobody will buy it, Sandy. They'll know it was you."

"No, I don't quite think so, Gerald. They'll think I'm out of here, gone to someplace like maybe Mexico. But they'll be very sad that the pressure of all the murder cases you've worked on—including mine—drove you into such a deep depression that you killed your whole family, then killed yourself. Now sit in that chair and say a prayer."

He resorted to begging. "Please...let my wife and kids alone. It will be punishment enough that they'll have to live without a father. They're totally innocent. They never wronged you in any way, Sandy."

"No human being on this earth is innocent!" she scoffed adamantly. "I loved my hogs far more than I could ever love a person! Now sit down and get ready to die, or I'll just start shooting at random."

Trying not to show how scared he was, he slowly did as he was told, and then she put the gun to his temple.

Jenny suddenly screamed and rushed at Sandy—but she clubbed Jenny to the floor with the gun barrel. Then the kids yelled and cried, running at Sandy and grabbing her legs—but they were no match for her, and she kicked them aside. She put the gun to Jerry's temple again while Jenny writhed and moaned on the floor and pulled the kids toward her and hugged them, wet with tears and knowing they were all going to die.

Sandy was smiling as her finger tightened on the trigger to blow Jerry's brains out.

BLAM! A tremendously loud shot rang out, reverberating in the small living room.

But it was *not* Jerry who got shot—it was Sandy. A bloody hole appeared in her forehead. Then she fell with a thud, dropping Jerry's weapon.

Vince Spivak stepped into the living room, his own gun in his hand, still smoking.

Jerry stared at him, aghast, then mumbled, "How in the world...how did you know...why are you here?"

"To save your life, so show some gratitude, Jerry. I don't know why, but I had a feeling I should drive over here just to check on you."

Jerry bent down to pull his wife and kids up from the floor, then cradled them in his arms. Billy and Janie were still whimpering, and Jenny looked very weak and disoriented.

Jerry said, "You're gonna be okay, honey, talk to me. Janie—Get an ambulance. You know how to call 9-1-1, don't you?"

"Yes, Daddy—but my phone's in my room 'cause Mom grounded me on it."

"Well, you're not grounded now. Hurry up!"

Billy said, "I'll get my phone, too!"

They both run upstairs.

Jenny seemed to be groggily coming around, and Jerry wiped her brow with his hand. Then he eyed Vince and said, "How could you have known what was going down here tonight?"

"Like I said, something was telling me I'd better keep a bit of a watch on your house while Little Miss Sandy was on the loose. Maybe I'm clairvoyant."

"More like obsessive-compulsive."

Jenny piped up, still sounding weak. "Thank God, Vince. You saved us."

Jerry said, "Why didn't you tell me what you were going to do, Vince?"

"Because you would've told me to back off. You always think you can handle anything that comes your way. That's how you got shot two years ago by that punk kid."

"He's right," Jenny softly chided. "You're too stubborn, honey."

Jerry kissed her forehead and said, "We better call Sheriff Patton and tell him to get here with the coroner and a couple of his men."

Vince stared down at Sandy's body and said, "A fitting end to her would be if she could be fed to her hogs."

The day after the attempted murders at the Delaneys' suburban home, Stacie Graver summed things up this way for her viewers:

"Sandy Jacobs, the trans woman serial killer popularly dubbed the Hog Lady, was buried today in a pauper's grave whose location is undisclosed, for fear that morbid trophy seekers would disturb it, seeking souvenirs of her evil exploits. It is suspected that the notorious Hog Lady could have paid for a lavish funeral with the money she stole over the years from her victims, but if so, the loot remains hidden somewhere, possibly in offshore bank accounts.

"Many opinion writers say that Sandy's pauper burial isn't a suitable end for a woman who treated the ones she killed with far less dignity. In any case, this seems to be the much hoped for finale to her gruesome story. But so far, there are at least a half dozen writers with books and screenplays in the works, so it seems that she might be as criminally legendary as Son of Sam or Jeffrey

Dahmer. Such is the way of our pervasively lurid society."

A LOOK AT: THE DARKEST WEB

John A. Russo, co-writer of the movie *Night of the Living Dead*, spins a tale of greed, corruption, and maliciously evil intent where anyone can become a victim...for the right price.

When Anthropology Professor Neville Pinnock, whose friend and mentor was murdered five years ago, teams up with Fiona Evans, whose sister has been recently murdered under similar circumstances, the stage is set for a showdown of biblically epic proportions. As Neville and Fiona wend their way through lies and deception in search of the truth, the pair encounter darkness and evil they could have never dared to believe is real.

From underground Dark Web sites, showcasing brutalities the likes of which has never been seen, to Manhattan boardrooms and basements concealing depravities of the foulest kind, Neville and Fiona find themselves in a battle for their very lives and souls.

Just when it seems like all is known, a twist of fate ramps up the terror even further...instilling dread until the very last page.

"An unrelieved orgy of sadism." —Variety **on** *Night of the Living Dead*

AVAILABLE NOW

ABOUT THE AUTHOR

With forty books published internationally and nineteen feature movies in worldwide distribution, John A. Russo has been called a "living legend." He began by co-authoring the screenplay for *Night of the Living Dead*, which has become recognized as a "horror classic." His three books on the art and craft of movie making have become bibles of independent production, and one of them, *Scare Tactics*, won a national award for Superior Nonfiction. Quentin Tarantino—and many other noted filmmakers—have stated that Russo's books helped them launch their careers.

John wants people to know he's just a nice guy who likes to scare people—and he's done it with novels and films such as *Return of the Living Dead, Midnight, The Majorettes, The Awakening, Heartstopper*, and *My Uncle John Is a Zombie*. He has had a long, rewarding career, and he shows no signs of slowing down.

One of his best novels, *Dealey Plaza*—dealing with the epidemic of gun violence in America—was published to great acclaim by Burning Bulb Publishing. His screenplay, *The Night They Came Home*, is a Western horror story based on true events, and is currently in production in California.

John's popularity among genre fans remains at a high pitch, and he appears at many movie conventions each year as a featured guest, where attendees are welcome to come to his table or the bar to share drinks, jokes, and serious conversation.

Made in United States
Troutdale, OR
12/18/2023

15984670R00130